THE TEXT BOOK AFFAIR

Copyright © 2016
By
ADAM CHRISTOPHER
Published by Attractive Mind Limited

For information contact: www.attractivemind.co.uk

Copyright Registration Receipt ID#
DEP636031572323987135
ISBN: 978-0-9955439-0-4
Second Edition: January 2017
10 9 8 7 6 5 4 3 2 1

Contents

CHAPTER ONE
Girl's Night Out

ONE FRIDAY NIGHT in September; "Don't look now! There's a bloke over there" giggled Kat, jerking her head to indicate the direction. "He keeps staring at you. Do you know him?" "Don't look, don't look!!" she squealed as Demi went to look. They laughed, took a swig of their drinks and laughed some more, as Demi gingerly turned her head in a hope of catching a glimpse without him spotting her looking.

It was a last minute 'girls from work' night out. Demi hadn't intended joining them as being the boss it didn't always seem right to be mixing outside work with just a few of the team.

Kat was Demi's closest work buddy. They had worked together in healthcare for eight years and had moved to their current roles at the same time 3 years before. Emma, Sarah and Val made up the group and they all enjoyed the occasional night out together. They were a good team ranging in age from 25 to 50.

Because Demi hadn't planned on joining them she was the only one still in business wear as the others had changed in the office before leaving. It was Friday night after all! As one of the eldest in the group, and the boss, Demi was feeling decidedly 'frumpy' in comparison with her colleagues and with other revellers who were out having a good time.

They had decided to head for a trendy part of town where they could get something to eat followed by a choice of up-market, social cosmopolitan places where they could go for a drink. They were out for a fun time and they were determined to make the best of it.

For early September it was a warm balmy evening and spirits were high, with most people having recently returned to work following their summer breaks.

As Demi turned her head and caught a glimpse she immediately recognised the 'bloke over there' as Kat had called him. Giggling and somewhat speechless she told Kat that she knew him and in a minute she would be able to recall his name. They had, by this time, had a few glasses of wine!!

"He's still looking, he's still looking" Kat kept squealing. "Do you think he'll come over?" Then, because she recognised him and wanted to make a good impression, Demi started to act more sensibly and with this she began to recall more details of who, where, when and what.

It wasn't long before Demi was able to tell Kat that his first name was Joshua and that his surname would come to her soon. She knew that it began with a B.

*

Demi recalled the last time that she and Josh had met.

Josh had been a Senior Manager within Financial Services when Demi first met him. This was about ten or eleven years before and as a Consultant in Human Resources Demi had supported him with recruitment and other staff issues. They had worked well together and had fun. Josh was actually considered to be the 'hot stuff' of the company. As they were both happily married at the time neither of them had even considered anything other than a work friendship based on mutual respect.

Josh was a young high flier. It was obvious he was 'going places' and that he would get there. He was dynamic, charming, charismatic, successful and stunning! Everyone enjoyed working with him and for him.

It had been strange then when one day, two years before that Friday night; completely unexpectedly, Josh had approached Demi in a coffee shop. The coffee shop was next door to where Demi worked and she often used it for meetings with members of her team. It was during one of these meetings when Josh approached her saying "its Demi, isn't it?" Looking up she had been startled to see the 'hot stuff' from the office standing there. He knew her name! Remembered her! As she caught her breath she managed to compose herself enough to reply "yes, ugh, Joshua, really lovely to see you." "I won't interrupt your meeting; it's good to see you too. Here's my business card. Call me, we'll get coffee." And he was gone.

Well, needless to say, Demi's colleague was flabbergasted, and after picking herself up off the floor, wanted all the gossip, ASAP. Unfortunately there wasn't any gossip. Demi put Joshua's business card in her purse and thought how he might be a good networking contact as she was about to start to look for her next career move. Nothing more than that, at that time, had crossed Demi's mind. She was, after all, still married at that point.

She had immediately noted that Josh's business card reflected his 'high flier' status. He was already the Chief Executive of a large Financial Services provider, Grants Holding.

And, this is where the story would have ended if it hadn't had been for that Friday girl's night out in September.

*

Emma was going to the bar for the next round of drinks. Demi offered to help, saying to Kat "I will remember his surname by the time I get back and then I will go up and say hello."

At the bar Demi told Emma what was going on and in doing so remembered that Josh's surname was Barnes. When they got back with the drinks Demi told Kat what she had remembered and as they looked around they realised that Josh had left the building. He was nowhere to be seen. Val even rushed outside to see if she could see where he and his mates were heading – nothing!

Oh well, thought Demi, it had been fun while it had lasted!

For some reason, that didn't stop Kat. She was on a roll. Now that she knew his name and where he worked she was straight on to Google. Due to the wine, thankfully for Demi, it was short lived and they all moved on to the next bar.

CHAPTER TWO
Weekend Fantasy

THE REST OF DEMI'S weekend was quiet, like so many before since her marriage break up 18 months ago. She had bought her lovely 2 bed, 2 bath flat almost a year ago that she shared with her son, Chas. Needless to say she spent a lot of time on her own as Chas, rightly so as a teenager, was only home for food, a shower and occasionally, a bed. Chas was a good lad, most of the time, as was Aaron, her eldest son. Aaron and his girlfriend, Nadia, had bought their own flat almost a year ago as well.

Throughout the weekend, with it being a quiet one, Demi's mind kept thinking back to Friday night. She couldn't get the picture of Josh out of it. While sitting at her computer doing research for a project she was working on she found herself googling the company Josh worked for and looking up his credentials. She still had his business card from two years before in her purse and she had used it to check him out.

He was still the CEO of Grants Holding and he also held a prestigious role at the financial services governing body in London. His work profile and achievements were outstanding. His photo did him justice and portrayed him as a 'dream come true'. Demi took time to fantasise and day dream about how he was everything any girl could desire, tall, dark and handsome; suave, sophisticated and charming; kind, caring and compassionate; sexy as hell and loaded!! What more was needed?

Decision made. Demi would call him at work on Monday from her office. It would be easy, he was a business contact and she could use this to good effect. It sounded simple. What had she got to lose? After all he would make a good business contact and according to google he was married to Angela and had two daughters. It would be good to catch up and add him to her network. Simple. What else would it be?

Monday, arriving at the office as usual, Demi settled at her desk. The only difference today was that Josh's business card had been placed neatly next to her phone as a reminder to ring him. She was determined to keep the courage from her weekend fantasising.

Every now and again Demi found herself staring at Josh's business card and day dreaming some more. Driving herself scatty she went off in search of Kat and the others to debrief from Friday night and share weekend adventures. She decided to keep quiet about her google findings and not to say anything about her plans to ring Josh. She didn't want to put herself under any more pressure.

The team were in good form and they had fun recounting their escapades of Friday night and the weekend. They teased her about the mystery 'hotty' and Kat threatened to do some research to find out more about him.

Demi just let the excited chatter go on, joining in where needed. She enjoyed her team. They were good colleagues who knew when and how to be professional and respectful and when it was ok to have a laugh. She had a good relationship with all of them and she enjoyed the experience and learning that they gave her every day.

Back in her office Demi had managed to convince herself that as CEO Josh was bound to have his own Secretary or PA. And, as she knew well, any good Secretary would only take a message from a new name phoning in. It was therefore highly unlikely that she would get to speak to him. This line of thought boosted Demi's confidence and gave her the added courage to pick up the phone.

"Good morning, Grants Holding." Demi was through to the switchboard and quickly finding her voice said "Eh, yes, good morning. Please can you put me through to Joshua Barnes?" Demi managed to compose herself enough and despite the nerves and croaky voice thought she had managed to sound very official. Then she heard a voice replying.

"Hello, Mr Barnes' Secretary."

Oh no! Now what? Thought Demi as panic consumed her. Pulling herself together she managed to speak again.

"Oh, hello. Please can I speak to Joshua?"

"I'm sorry, Mr Barnes is on holiday." Came the answer. Well, that took the wind out of Demi's sails for a moment or two!

Gathering herself she quickly asked, "Ok, when is he due back?" "In two weeks." The Secretary replied. "Ok" said Demi "I'll call back, thank you." And she hung up.

With her heart racing Demi was very excited by the fact that she had the courage to phone, yet feeling disappointed that Josh hadn't been there. Now, she would have to do it all again in two weeks' time. Would she? Could she find the courage to do it all again?

Feeling full of bravery Demi went through to tell the others what she had done. Keeping the story intense before dropping the bombshell of Josh being on holiday.

CHAPTER THREE
Fun While it Lasted

FINALLY THE WAITING was over. Would she or wouldn't she? It had been a long two weeks and Demi's courage had been wavering one minute and strengthening the next. Again, Josh's business card was placed on her desk next to her phone, in readiness.

This time Demi knew Josh was more than likely to be in the office. Would she get past the Secretary? What if she did? She wouldn't. At best she would leave a message and then have to wait to see whether he would ever ring back. What if he didn't ring back? How long would she give it before ringing again? Would she ring again? Oh, oh, it was all too much. She was scaring herself.

Demi stood up; a change of scene was needed. Some light relief for a few minutes would help her to calm down, refocus and rebuild her courage. She went in search of Kat and the others.

Half an hour later, back in her office and feeling brave Demi picked up the phone, held her breath and dialled the number.

"Good Morning, Grants Holding." It already sounded familiar. Realising she needed to breath before she could speak she let out a big sigh. "Sorry" she said quickly and then composing herself said "Joshua Barnes please." "Yes, certainly, I'll put you through."

"Hello, Josh speaking." Panic struck. Oh no! How did that happen? And then, like a person possessed words spilled out of her mouth and she couldn't stop herself.

"Hello, Joshua its Demi, Demi Ryan. I saw you in town a couple of weeks ago and you were looking across at me. I couldn't remember your name and didn't want to speak to you until I did and when I did you were gone and I thought I would ring you to apologise for not speaking to you and to see how you are and to catch up." Breathe!

The words just tumbled out of her mouth before she had time to think. What a mess! So much for wanting to show him how professional and successful she was.

"Hey, Demi, it's good to speak to you." How calm and sophisticated he sounded. "How did you get my number?" Oh, no! Now she would have to tell him that she had held onto his business card for years. How uncool and stalker-ish was that?

"Oh" she said. "Remember we bumped into each other a couple of years ago and you gave me your business card? Well I remembered where you worked from that and followed a hunch." Well done! That didn't sound too bad, did it?

Then, suddenly it seemed that it was his turn to lose his nerve as he began to say how he had left his wife recently, she had been leading a double life and things had become very difficult. His wife had organised an attack on him with a knife and he had sought safe housing. He had two daughters, the eldest of whom was living with him now and the youngest who was living with her Mum. Life was a mess and he was getting through it as best he could. He said how wonderful it was to talk and perhaps they could meet for coffee sometime. He then said "What's your number? I'll call you."

Without thinking of any possible negative consequences Demi gave Josh her mobile number straight away. The call ended and Demi put the phone down, adrenalin making her shake, giggle and go giddy all at once.

Phew! She was exhausted! And excited!! Suddenly thinking, why hadn't she kept it professional and given him her work number? Oh, no! What now? She ran into the next office to find Kat. She couldn't help the biggest grin taking over her face.

"You'll never guess what I've just done?" She giggled, hopping from one foot to the other in excitement.

"What, what?" Chimed Kat, immediately joining in with the fun.

"I just spoke to him."

"Who?"

"Josh, you know the man from the other night."

"You haven't? When? What did he say?" Kat was on the edge of her seat seeking all the gory details and fast. She couldn't believe Demi could have done this. Wow, Kat was impressed. Demi was so brave.

Demi filled Kat in with all the details and they were both excited. Emma, who had joined in with the conversation on her return from a meeting, was also jumping up and down with excitement. It was 'sensible' Val who brought them all back to earth when she said "So, what happens next? How did you leave it with him?" That knocked the wind out of their sails!

Feeling sheepish Demi repeated that she had given him her number and he had said he would call sometime. They all knew then that this was probably wishful thinking as he was unlikely to call and that would be the end of that.

Oh well! Thought Demi again, it was fun while it lasted!

*

That afternoon Demi had settled down and was in her office finalising a report for a Board meeting later in the week. She had a couple of meetings later in the afternoon and she needed to get this report finished beforehand. It should have been in last Friday only the Secretaries had allowed her a deadline extension because they knew how busy she was and they liked her.

Demi had been asked to take on the role of Acting Director to cover maternity leave. She had covered the role before so knew what it would be like and she had plenty of experience. She also enjoyed the additional pressure and responsibility; and the extra pay was an added bonus. She had a great reputation and she was ready to take her next career move. This opportunity of covering the Director role for a few months would definitely help her achieve this dream.

She was in a good place in her life. Single, own property, nice car and two lovely boys. She was a free spirit, which would give her plenty of flexibility when looking for her new role. She could work anywhere and would rent a property close to her employer to enable her to commute weekly.

As usual Demi's desk was incredibly tidy and organised. Colleagues would often comment on it. Demi knew where everything was and everything had its place. She didn't believe in having a tray for filing and spending hours every couple of weeks putting it away. There was no need, as she saw it. If something was important enough to keep then it was kept with the papers it needed to be kept with, straight away. That way, if she needed a file she knew it would always have the latest information in it and there was nothing she could miss that might otherwise be in the depths of a filing tray somewhere.

On her desk that afternoon and as usual for Demi when working there, was her lipstick, in its lipstick case (a girlie item that she was never without) and her mobile phone.

Unlike most other senior managers and Directors, Demi's phone was not an appendage. In fact she disliked the way they had become a distraction and a disruption. In her view they had their place for emergencies and for ease of communication and for her there was a time and a place, which was not at work. Consequently, it wasn't unusual for Demi to go all day without making or receiving calls or texts. And, as she also didn't use it for social media or emails, it rarely made a noise. This suited Demi fine and was why, when suddenly in the middle of being lost in her report writing, she jumped a mile when her phone 'pinged' to indicate that a text message had arrived.

Feeling cross at the intrusion Demi stared at the phone and then ignored it for as long as she could. When she couldn't stand the not knowing any longer she slowly picked it up with a big sigh. It was most likely one of her boys wanting a lift somewhere or her Mum checking to make sure she was still alive, berating her for not being in touch for ages – didn't she realise how busy she was?

Feeling slightly irked for being disturbed she opened the text. It was from a number her phone didn't recognise. It read:

Hi good to hear from you today – glad that my business card survived the test of time!! J☺

Her stomach did a flip and Demi jumped up without another thought about her report. OMG! What was she going to do now? She must stay calm. Act normal, professional and........breathe!

Where was Jenny when she needed her? Jenny was much better at this sort of thing. Demi wasn't used to flirting, being casual or whatever it was called these days. She had, of course, being female, already had their future mapped out. Text, coffee, dinner, romantic liaison, relationship, happily ever after. Wasn't that how it went?

Jenny was Demi's best friend. They met when working for Insurance 4 U, which is where Demi had first met Josh. Jenny also knew Josh although she hadn't worked with him like Demi had. Jenny was from South Africa, although she had been born in the UK. Her parents emigrated with her and her brother when she was two years old. Like so many others before her, she had returned to the UK to find fame and fortune. With the grass always being greener.

Jenny had returned to South Africa 18 months ago to be closer to her family. As, apart from owning a property and for Demi, there was nothing else for Jenny in the UK. She had split from her long term boyfriend a couple of years before and she had become disillusioned with her career. South Africa was where her heart was and the pull to return was stronger than her desire to stay in the UK.

Demi missed her lots. She had visited her for a month a year ago and they were planning Demi's second trip for February next year. They were both very excited and couldn't wait. It seemed like ages away.

Demi had already told Jenny about seeing Josh at the girl's night out and about the phone call to his office a couple of weeks before. Jenny had been encouraging and had said that Demi must call him again. Jenny will be surprised when she hears what's happened now. She will not believe that Demi has been brave enough to call again and she will scream with excitement about the text.

Demi focused on the next dilemma. How long should she leave it before she replied? Too quick might seem too keen and too slow might seem like she's not interested. Oh, why wasn't there any guidance manual on this sort of thing? How was she supposed to know what to do?

Demi decided to email Jenny giving her an update and seeking her advice on a reply. Kat and the others had all gone off to various meetings and Demi found herself alone with her dilemma. She herself had a meeting to go to in an hour and a report to finish.

After emailing Jenny, Demi decided to get on and finish her report. Hopefully, this would take her mind off things for a while.

CHAPTER FOUR
Unconventional

WITH THE REPORT finished and emailed off at last, Demi checked to see if Jenny had replied. As there had been no reply from Jenny yet meant that she must be in a meeting. Demi couldn't bear to wait any longer. She needed to get this done. She would have to go with her own instincts. It was mid-afternoon; if she got on with it she could send a reply to Josh before her next meeting. If she didn't do it now she wouldn't get chance until much later that evening and that might appear rude. Not only that, she couldn't bear the thought of spending the rest of the day thinking about her reply. After a bit of deliberation and with shaking fingers she finally settled for:

Who said it was your business card that I remembered? If you fancy a drink sometime give me a call. Dx

And pressed send.

She wasn't sure about the X. Maybe she should have done a smiley? Thing was, she didn't know what she was supposed to do and there was no-one around to ask! Another thing she did was save his mobile number in her contacts so that she would know if he called or sent a text again.

When she finally got home that evening Demi was shattered. It had been a long day and with the added excitement the adrenalin had tired her out. She poured a large glass of wine and proceeded to cook pasta for one, which she would eat in front of the TV watching her favourite soaps. She found this the perfect way to unwind these days. Just as she settled down and was reflecting on her day her mobile 'pinged' indicating the arrival of a text message.

She was surprised and very excited to see that it was from Josh. She hadn't expected to hear from him quite so soon and in any event had thought that he would call if anything as that was what her text had suggested. Noticing her pulse beginning to race and with trembling fingers, Demi opened his message.

Crumbs I know my interview techniques were unconventional but I didn't realise just how bad I was for you to remember after all these years!!!☺

This made Demi laugh out loud. He was flirting with her for sure. Now she needed to think of a fun reply, and she wanted to know how to do 'smilies'. Shortly after receiving the text Demi's youngest son Chas arrived home. After some casual conversation she asked him how to do 'smilies' on her phone and also took the opportunity to find out a bit more about various symbols. It was all a bit 'technical' and as usual Demi didn't do 'technical' - she just didn't get what all the fuss was about. Anyway, she now knew how to do a smiley face at least.

It had got quite late by this time and it didn't feel appropriate to send a text reply after 10pm. Not only that she was tired and ready for bed. She would reply after she got to work in the morning. That would give her time to think of a witty response with maybe some flirting, if she was brave enough. After a restless night and various thoughts about what to text back Demi finally arrived at work and went with:

Your theory on unconventional being bad is a good discussion topic. And who said that it was your interviewing techniques that I remembered?☺☺

Note the two 'smilies' for good measure! It had taken Demi about 45 minutes to write this text and press send. All the time her pulse was racing, she couldn't stop smiling and her hands were shaking. What was happening to her? Usually she was strong, confident and professional and these couple of texts and one phone call were sending her all sorts of strange feelings and emotions, that if she admitted it, she quite liked.

All day she kept checking her phone for a reply – nothing. Had she offended him? Did he not get her sense of humour? Oh well, it was only a couple of texts and had been fun while it had lasted. At least he'd made her pulse race and brought a smile to her face.

Back home and still no reply, she had just about given up hope and moved on when from the lounge she heard her mobile buzzing in the kitchen. She jumped up and quickly ran to check it. Could it be from him?

I know I wore some horrendous ties in those days but I didn't realise they were quite that memorable!!☺..........

Hey, he got it and was able to return an equally witty reply. Then came the bombshell!

..........D – I'm finding my feet again after 25 years out and things have changed!! I'd have loved to go for a drink as your texts really make me laugh and I could sure do with a few laughs. I've just asked someone out who surprisingly said yes and want to make a go of it – I'm a bit old fashioned and don't want to mess anyone about! Given my recent luck I'll soon no doubt find out they are an axe wielding maniac!! If you're not put off I'd like to keep in touch even if it's so that you can remind me how obnoxious I was all those years ago!!☺

Devastated!! Demi's reply would need to be good and not show her disappointment. Definitely a glass of wine was required to enable deployment of her best selected words – ever! For sure this would be the last text from him so even more important for her to get the sentiment in balance with humour. Two hours later – and send..................

I'm really pleased for you. She is a lucky woman. Thanks for letting me know and absolutely happy to keep in touch for old time's sake. And who said it was the ties?

She was very pleased with herself. She had kept professional and risen above her own disappointment. Her only dilemma had been what she should do with smiley faces and other punctuation marks – she really had a lot to learn when it came to text protocol. In this instance she decided it was best to leave them out just in case she got it completely wrong and sent something that meant something very different in text language!

She had made a friend if nothing else, which felt good. What would Kat say tomorrow when Demi updated her? What would Jenny say? Demi would email her first thing. Demi was planning how she could relay the story and maintain a careless attitude when really there was a tinge of sadness in her heart. She would have really loved it if things could have been different. It was a long night – again.

The next morning Demi arrived at work and set about her usual routine. As she got her mobile out of her bag to put on her desk she noticed she had a text message. Convinced it would be from anyone other than Josh she opened it with a heavy sigh.

Well now I'm struggling......... Not the interviewing techniques or ties......... Perhaps the 80's style "dynasty" look-a-like flared suits must have left their mark!!! J☺

With her heart pounding she couldn't help laughing out loud. What a fantastic morning tonic. Conscious that she would be stuck in meetings most of the day she wanted to reply quickly to keep him interested. That way he might text again later. Not only that, if she did reply quickly then it would be his turn to respond.

Who's Mark? Was he in Dynasty??

Was the best she could do – quickly! Was it too cryptic this time? She had enjoyed sending it. What would he think? Would this make him laugh? Suddenly Demi felt responsible for his emotions and good mood.

Luckily Demi hadn't emailed Jenny yet. What a story this would be now. Demi partly wished she had taken time to ask Jenny about how to reply as she was worried she had been too cryptic and was now concerned that she may have put him off. Next time she wouldn't rush, if there was a next time!

It was ages before Demi finally caught up with Kat and when she relayed the story Kat had found the whole saga hysterically funny. She was stunned that Demi had even made contact let alone carried on sending texts. Kat also felt a bit sorry that Josh was already in a relationship as Demi could do with a bit of fun.

As time passed with no response Demi became more and more cross with herself for rushing a reply. She wouldn't do that again that's for sure.

It was 5 days later and she had received nothing. It was hell. Should she apologise? Should she send another text? If so, what should she write?

Oh well, maybe this was really the end now. 'Fun while it lasted' she reminded herself with a sigh. Onwards and upwards.

CHAPTER FIVE
Rapper MC

HAVING USED THE weekend to pull herself together and get her emotions back in balance Demi was ready to take on another busy week. Maybe she would call Josh in a couple of weeks, maybe she wouldn't. She still had a business networking excuse she could use. After all that had been her intention for contacting him in the first place, hadn't it?

Her weekend had been a good tonic. Spending it with her family they had travelled to Bridgwater, staying overnight for her cousin's big birthday party. They had a lovely time and being close friends, having grown up together and their children also growing up together, they had talked, drunk, and danced the weekend away. Demi had not had much time to dwell on the events of Josh, which had been helpful in moving her emotions on.

Then back at work Monday morning, feeling confident and in control Demi opened a text message without considering who it might have been from.

Hi, how was your weekend? Wondered if you'd seen the brawl in town on Saturday night and if you were ok??!! Have a good week.☺

Oh, my goodness! Where had that come from? Demi was back to square one emotionally and clearly too delirious to think clearly, replying straight away.

If that's a summary of your weekend then I'm sorry to hear it. I spent the weekend in Bridgwater for my 'older' cousin's big birthday. It was lots of fun. Hope you had a good time with the new date. Have a good week too. D☺

Wow!! So much for not rushing to respond. Excitement had got the better of her and she had thrown all caution to the wind. Luckily though Demi didn't have to wait long for a reply.

I've heard that Bridgwater is rocking this time of year!! Had a rather eventful weekend....... Went for a walk along the beach! Forgot about the nudist section!! Date wasn't very impressed..... I was hellishly embarrassed!! Bit of a cock up so to speak! Board week, in name and nature!!! Have a good one.☺

Whoops! Demi found this very funny. Date must be a real prude if she hadn't firstly, known where the nudist part of the beach was and secondly, hadn't found it hilarious when stumbling across it. At least Josh had managed to maintain a sense of humour in his portrayal of his weekend.

She could empathise with Josh's comments regarding Board week. It was the same with her and most other large organisations where the Board of Executive and Non-Executive Directors meet monthly to discuss business strategy. Often these meetings were as dull as ditch water and only took place to comply with Corporate Governance. Demi had a busy morning and with everything going on at work it was late morning before she had chance to compose a reply.

Fancy exposing the new date to that!! Board week here too. Where does it state in a NEDs job description that they must be old, fat and grumpy, because they all are!! D☺

When Demi had researched Josh's organisation she had seen photos and read synopsis of all his NEDs (Non-Executive Directors) so she knew that he would understand her comments. She was also aware that his week, like hers, would be very full-on with finalising and reading Board papers along with all the 'off the record' talks and corridor conversations that were needed to steer the business transactions.

Therefore, when she hadn't received a reply by the end of the day, she wasn't surprised. Demi had already decided that if she hadn't received anything from Josh by Friday then she would text him again to see how his week had been and see what he was up to at the weekend. After all they were only just becoming new friends and didn't need to be texting everyday like love sick teenagers!

It was late Friday afternoon before Demi had chance to draw breath. She had managed to get her usual coffee from the Canteen on her way back to her office after another long day of meetings. Demi decided that she would have a few minutes to relax before facing the ever growing pile of paperwork on her desk that needed to be sorted before she went home.

This breather allowed her mind to wander to Josh and she wondered how his week had panned out. She decided to text him to find out before she changed her mind and talked herself out of it.

Phew! What a week. Just finishing some admin before heading home and looking forward to pouring a large glass of wine when I get there.☺☺ So what liberating plans are you exposing to the new date this weekend? Actually, probably best you don't answer that!! Whatever your plans hope you have fun. D☺

With that, smiling to herself, Demi faced the paperwork challenge. Lost in thought she was woken from her day dreams by the sound of her mobile 'pinging' with a text message. Wow, that was too quick to be Josh. Must be one of the boys, she thought.

Hey you was just thinking about texting to see how you got on with your fat NEDs!! Saying that I've got through 7 cakes today all for a great cause mind you!! Ohh and I had 5 choco mints to wash them down with!! There is something to be said for losing a stone after a messy divorce!! I've got one last meeting tonight then I'm free!! Going suit shopping with my daughter in the City so going to end up looking like a blooming rapper or worse after she's done her makeover on me!! Have a good one and don't talk to too many strange men (apart from me that is).☺

Oh boy! Why did he have to have a new girlfriend? Demi sighed. She could easily fall in love with this man just from the tone of his texts. Here he was sharing her humour and bearing some personal issues along with taking ownership of her well-being with a show of gentle protection. How kind, caring and romantic. This time she definitely needed to think before sending a suitable reply. She pushed her papers to one side and started to write out her response. After several attempts and not being able to concentrate, she decided to wait until she got home before finishing it and pressing send.

How many cakes? And 5 choc mints! What was it, the Joshua Barnes 'expand the middle' charity? Careful or you could end up as one of those fat, grumpy NEDs. Talking of which, fat NEDs getting antsy over possible legal action they know nothing about is enough to turn any saint into a sinner. Anyway all pales into insignificance after driving home, roof down, in glorious sunshine and while sitting on my veranda with a large glass of wine, breathing in fresh sea air – oh, then I woke up!! Hope you enjoy being 'free' and your shop with your daughter sounds like fun. They'll be calling you MC Suit on Monday.☺

As Demi had been typing her text she realised that the piece about having the roof down and glass of wine on the veranda sounded a bit pretentious, despite the fact that it was true. So she thought she would pretend that it was only a dream as in truth there was nothing glamorous about her convertible car and her small, scruffy veranda that only caught about two hours max of the late afternoon sun. She hoped that she had managed to strike the right balance and share some humour with some personal bits enough to show him that she was interested.

The weekend came and went. Demi hadn't really expected to get another text from Josh. After all he was busy shopping and had his daughter and girlfriend to entertain.

That didn't mean that she hadn't thought about him. He was constantly in her thoughts. She was always wondering what he was doing and whether he would be interested in what she was doing. She also day dreamed about what she would be doing differently if he were with her. Demi had explained all about Josh to her sister Jaini while they were out shopping. They had a lovely time, as always, as they were very close and spent a lot of time together. Jaini had two girls and over the years they had taken advantage of sharing their children. The four cousins also enjoyed each other's company.

CHAPTER SIX
International Man of Mystery

MONDAY MORNING, 6am and the alarm was sounding. Demi reached over, turned it off and headed for the shower. In the process of getting ready for work she was surprised to receive a text message so early. It could only be from her friend Jenny in South Africa. Being two hours ahead, Jenny was probably at work already! Demi opened the text.

Hi how was your weekend?? Not too much posing with the roof down I hope?? Don't call me 'pale face'! I had to endure 2 days of shopping as my eldest daughter gave me a fashion makeover such that I'm now as you say MC Suit!! Mind you think I should have washed this new shirt before putting it on this morning....Bit sensitive on the old bits.....Guess it's the starch!☺

What an early morning tonic! Demi found this very funny and it made her warm and giggly inside. She wished she could be with him so that they could share closely the fun they were having.

Demi decided, against her previous self-promise, to go for a quick reply. She knew she had meetings as soon as she got to work and it would be lunchtime before she had another chance and she didn't want to keep him waiting that long. Also, there were so many opportunities for a very flirty response that it was better that she didn't give it too much thought!!

MC Suits you Sir! Sounds like you had a good time even if you are left with some sensitive parts today!! My weekend was quiet. Went self-indulgent shopping and DIY shopping on Saturday then paperwork and housework Sunday. The only strange man I spoke to was in the DIY shop about my paint unless you count my 2 sons as I actually saw both of them at various points and they can be a bit 'strange' (as well as lovely) at times!! Any fat NEDs on the agenda this week? Enjoy your week. D☺

Not her best effort. Never mind it would have to do!

Just as she was locking her front door to head to her car and drive to work she heard her phone 'ping' as a new text arrived. In a hurry, and knowing that it couldn't possibly be from Josh, it would have to wait until she got to work.

It was 7.45am before she arrived at her desk and her first meeting was at 8.15am. This gave her half an hour to sort papers, switch her computer on and check for any urgent emails. And get coffee! As she started to get organised she remembered the text message that she hadn't viewed yet. Hoping it would be quick one she opened it.

Hey you. You sure know how to rave at the weekends!! No fat NEDs this week.....on the silly o'clock to my second job with 'nerds' rather than NEDs at the 'land that time forgot' otherwise known as the IBSA this morning!! Got to have a boring suit and white shirt for the occasion!! Needless to say I don't comply. I'm in Wales later in the week and travelling around the Midlands next week. They don't call me 'international man of mystery' for nothing you know!!!☺

Damn that girlfriend! This was a man Demi really wanted to get to know. She was already in love with the man behind the texts. He made her feel warm and filled her with smiles and giggles. These simple texts stayed with her for days making her smile and crave his company, feeding her thoughts and fuelling her dreams.

Bringing herself quickly out of her day dreaming Demi remembered that she didn't have much time if she wanted to respond before mid-day. Hadn't he mentioned he was on the train? If she replied now she might still catch him before he reached the office. She would have to go with another quick one and hope for the best that she could do it justice this time.

Queen of the ravers me! I'm sure you'll wow the socks off the nerds (that's if they are wearing any) looking dapper in your new suit or should that be Dappy – you might need to ask your daughter to explain that one!☺ Wales should be fun, not sure about some of the places in the Midlands! International man of mystery or MC Suit – which one has the most charm, I wonder! Have fun. D☺

Would that be it now or would there be a reply. She guessed he could be at work already and would probably not get chance to send anything. She must remember that while he was uppermost in her mind, (she didn't have a lot else to get excited about) she was not going to be uppermost in his. After all, he had his daughter and a girlfriend and a very highly pressurised job. The fact that he had thought of her first thing on a Monday morning (Ok, she knew that he was on a long train journey and bored!) was something to be both pleased and excited about. And she was. For the moment that was good enough for her.

Demi's day was bright and breezy and she walked around on a high. It was amazing how a bit of fun and attention was lifting her spirits and giving her something to day dream and fantasise over, putting a real spring in her step.

As the week continued without a reply, Demi wondered whether she should take the lead and text him again. Now she was in a dilemma. If she sent another text would he think she was chasing him or would he think she was being 'friendly'? She put herself in his shoes. What would she think if he kept texting her? She convinced herself that she wouldn't mind and would enjoy it. Then that's what she would say, wouldn't she? Oh dear, this wasn't easy. How could she go from being so excited one minute to being so perplexed and worried the next? Her emotions would be stretched too far if this went on for too long. She would have to settle for believing that he was busy and that he would text again when he had another quiet moment.

Come Friday evening she couldn't take it any longer. She had managed to get home at a reasonable time, had eaten and was drinking her first glass of wine. Feeling brave she decided to text. What was the worst that could happen? She asked herself. Well, came the answer, he may not text back and if he didn't then where was the harm? It was, after all, only a new friendship that had no strings or promises, even if it was fun and the best thing that had happened to her for a while, a long while.

This week's carousel is just about to stop and I'm about to step off! Phewie!! Will be stepping on to the weekend one with a large glass of wine any minute now.☺ How about you? How was Wales? D☺

She didn't need to let on that she had already had one large glass of wine and was, by now, very settled into her second!

The big question was, would he reply? Or was he busy entertaining his 'girlfriend'. Grrrr!

Demi couldn't help it. Every few minutes she kept checking her phone for his text. All day Saturday she did her best to find things to do to take her mind of him, yet she still kept checking her phone. So much so that even her son commented on it when she was out for coffee with him!!

Apart from the girls at work, Jenny in South Africa and her closest colleague and friend Dyna, Demi hadn't told anyone else about Josh. She had decided to only tell Jaini in her family as no-one else needed to know and there was very little that Demi and Jaini didn't tell each other. Jaini could be trusted to keep a secret. What was there to tell anyone anyway? He was just another friend and her family didn't know all her friends, so why should Josh be so special?

By the time it got to 5pm on Saturday Demi had almost stopped checking her phone and had convinced herself that she wouldn't hear from Josh again. Why would he bother with her anyway? He was a busy, charismatic, high profile chap with lots of friends, family and acquaintances who needed his attention. And, remember, he had a girlfriend!

So, when her phone 'pinged' with a message alert she scrambled to it, pausing momentarily with nervous anticipation before opening it.

Hey u sorry I've been so long getting back to u but prat that I am left my phone on charge at my desk in the office! Good job I work 7 days a week so I found it this afternoon only after a good old bloke style panic!! Maybe I should pop over and see your memory loss specialists! Anyway every time you text you're just having another glass of wine! Something you want to tell me? Been working on slides for a couple of presentations I've got to do next week. Then over to Lyme Regis tomorrow to get my old Insurance 4 U chum to help me type them up....... Weekend what weekend! Off to the gym tonight (yes Saturday night) boy do I know how to let my hair down? How's your weekend going?☺

Did he ever let up? Where was his girlfriend in all of this? Demi was feeling responsible for him again. She also wanted to get closer to him so that she could really show him how life could be different. Give him a good reason for balancing his work and home life better. She decided her reply should be fun, supportive and maybe bring a bit of risqué into it. Clearly his 'girlfriend' wasn't able to distract him enough.

Typical bloke! Lost without a good women and/or PA.☺ All work and no play makes Josh a dull boy! Would love to be going to the gym only have to give it a miss for another week while I finish sorting my back out – don't ask!! Hence the wine – medicinal.☺☺ Memory loss specialist – is that what they call it now? Have done a few chores today and modelling in a fashion show tomorrow. Lyme Regis is a long way to go for a typist. She must be good!☺ Have fun. D☺

That caught his attention!

Blimmy intriguing!! So now you're a cat walk model!! I'll deny it if you ever bring it up down the cattle market (town centre) but I've done all my laundry, cleaning and washed the car today!! Modern man alive and kicking.....Haven't yet got in to the swing of my new life so couldn't face a night in ironing on my own so going to the gym as I don't know what to do with myself (see I said I was a 'saddo' really!!) Work, gym and cleaning......tell me that there is more to life than this before I go mad!!!! Actually don't comment on the go mad bit!!!☺

Demi felt compelled to respond quickly hoping to keep the fun going for as long as possible. He was obviously still hurting from his marriage breakup and in need of some light relief to get him through the 'dark' times. There she went again – always wanting to care and help. She really did want to get to know this guy better and having just a text relationship wasn't going to do it for her. However, she was prepared to play the game for a while to give him time. She wondered, briefly, about his girlfriend and where she was in his life.

Clearly as a women I do all of those things without thinking! However for a new 'modern' man you're sounding pretty good at it and your secret may be safe with me! At least you've got the gym to escape to, as sad as that maybe, I've only got Xfactor to look forward to – how's that in the 'saddo' competition stakes!☺ There is definitely more to life, you just need to let yourself find it and sometimes its right under your nose and you just need a little push. That's the philosophy over! It's a women's prerogative to be intriguing – never judge a book by its cover!! If you fancy sharing a bottle of wine sometime I'm sure I can find another glass! Enjoy the gym. D☺

Would he take her up on her offer of a glass of wine? Or better still would he get the subtle hint that it was her she was referring to in the subtext of being 'right under your nose'?

It wasn't until after she had made dinner, poured a glass of wine and fallen under the Xfactor spell that her phone 'pinged' to indicate a reply.

Ok ok you win the first round of the SSS (Sad Saturday night Syndrome) – however I'm coming back with a vengeance to win the final round... Ironing whilst eating Christmas cake!!! Enjoy Xfactor I hear it's quite racy!☺

Wow, he let me win! Well the first round anyway. And he's already started the next round. This is so much fun! She waited a short while before replying. Not too long as the excitement was getting the better of her.

Thought about letting you win just to be nice. Then thought better of it! How about ironing while singing Auld Lang Syne? Think that makes me the winner of the final, final round!☺ Xfactor is only racy if you're 16! Strictly is more my style. ☺

Would she get a reply tonight or had he gone off to the gym before getting ready to spend time with his 'girlfriend'. By the next morning Demi had already over thought the situation and believed she knew exactly what he was doing, who he was doing it with and what he was thinking. And had convinced herself that the 'girlfriend' had obviously spent the night and they had gone out for a romantic breakfast before going to Lyme Regis to see his ex-Insurance 4 U chum, as otherwise Demi was sure Josh would have replied by now.

By the time it had got to Sunday evening Demi could wait no longer for his reply. She had decided that it was possible that the ex-Insurance 4 U chum in Lyme Regis Josh had referred to was actually the 'girlfriend', which is why he was going there and spending the day.

Despite all of these negative thoughts Demi's positive ego managed to convince her that it would be ok to send another text. After all she had a story that she wanted to share with him that she had spent all day planning the words for. What if he thought she was chasing him? Came the retort from her negative ego.

Keeping some sense of balance she rationalised that it was only a text and he could choose whether to respond or not – couldn't he? Being unable to contain herself any longer she wrote her story:

Guess you're sulking cos you got beat! Either that or you're plotting the next round and I'm suitably scared.☺ Got reminded at 7.30 this morning of the worst thing about being "home alone". I was joined in my bedroom by an 8 legged "friend"!! Dilemma A) do I leave it till later? No as if not there when I get back I'll have to search for it. B) Do I wake my son to rescue me? No as he didn't get home till 4am and I probably won't be able to wake him anyway! C) Ring my other son to drive over and rescue me? No as he probably would be quite expletive! Nothing else for it, I would have to do it myself. Well I thought. I beat a 2 legged one yesterday so what's a few more legs to worry about.☺☺ Hope you've managed to sort your presentation slides and will get a few hours "play time" before tomorrow. D☺

She thought she had done a good job of keeping her text light and fun with just a bit of compassion at the end to show she cared. Would he notice? Would he respond? Yes!! Almost three hours later!!!!

Hiya sorry just got back from Lyme Regis – 3 of us been on my presentation slides since 2.30pm!! How did your catwalk experience go???? I guess I'm winning the Saddo stakes again as got woken twice last night by my daughter. The one with no keys!! Anyway got my revenge by going running at 7.30 this morning (when you were doing your hunting the insect bit!) – didn't seem to wake her up so came back and did my washing!! Have a great week.☺

Three of them? Must have been the 'girlfriend and the Insurance 4 U chum. Hummph!!! Was Demi jealous? Yes, maybe, a little! He does seem to be being put through the mill with his daughter and his apparent compulsion with the washing. Wishing me a great week already was suggesting that there would be no more texts until at least Friday. How could she wait that long??

CHAPTER SEVEN
Uptown Boy

MAYBE IF SHE pretended she was busy and waited until the morning before replying it would keep the magic alive for a bit longer. She didn't like it now when she was waiting for him to reply as she kept thinking about him and day dreaming about what he was doing and who he was doing it with.

Somehow Demi had to find out about the 'girlfriend' so that she could test out how flirty she could be in her messages and if there was any chance of pushing their friendship on to the next level.

In Demi's dreams and imagination the girlfriend was not happy and the relationship was coming to an end. Josh wasn't showing her enough interest and was distracted, not just by his divorce, by another woman who he insisted was just a 'friend'. The 'girlfriend' was jealous of his 'friend'. Demi enjoyed these day dreams.

In her other dreams Josh and his 'girlfriend' were very happy and she understood how caring and loving he was and how he shared that around his family and friends. The 'girlfriend' also knew how Josh 'humoured' this 'stalker' who had recently contacted him and how he treated the 'stalker' gently knowing that it would end soon. Of course, this dream had Demi as the 'stalker' and was her negative ego doing its worst. This dream always left Demi feeling hurt and sad.

Demi did her best to shake this off and to move her imagination under the control of her positive ego believing that one day soon they would be meeting for coffee. She would begin to see images of them laughing together and enjoying each other's company. On a good day this dream would continue by showing them spending the day, evening, night and whole weekend together. Finally morning arrived and Demi was able to bring herself into reality. Getting out of bed she was ready to plan, write and re-write her reply.

And just before her week was about to get busy she pressed the send button.

Ok I'll let u win that round! Please can I have 10 points in the bravery stakes for dealing with my 8 legged "friend"? Well done for getting your slides sorted. Good luck with the presentations – break a leg as they say in showbiz!☺ I'm sure you'll "knock 'em dead". Catwalk was great thanks. Amazing what cement, padded bra and spandex can do!! Enjoy the Midlands. D☺

This time Demi decided she would not, if she could resist, send another text unless she heard from him first. She must ease back on the chasing so as to give him chance to breathe. That way Demi would be able to see if Josh was keen or whether he was acting under pressure from her.

This decision led to a whole week of anticipation; of constantly checking and re-checking her phone for messages. Checking to make sure it was working and testing it by phoning it and texting it from other phones. Even the usual Friday night one didn't arrive. Demi held on to her resolve and resisted temptation to text. Her mind going over and over whether she should or shouldn't. For the sake of her own self-preservation she held strong.

Then, finally, Saturday morning and the wait was over....

Hi. How was your week? J

It might have only been one line! That was all it needed to set Demi off on another breathless rollercoaster. Being so excited and unable to take a chilled laid back approach she replied immediately.

It was good thanks. How about yours with your "jet setting" around the country? How did the presentation(s) go? I'm sure the audience were putty in your hands in no time. D☺

She even managed to keep her reply short to match his. He was obviously in the mood for some small talk as it wasn't long before he replied.

Absolutely shattered after my northern tour!!! Did my socialist presentation on Thursday and my capitalist one on Friday!!! Just off to town in my daughter's mobile disco (mini) for some shopping!! Ohh joy!!☺

Shopping, this early? He really must be an addict!

Does that mean you will be taking at least a few hours off this weekend to recharge the batteries? I'm off shopping with my niece and 7 month old great nephew this morning and then shopping with my son's fiancée this afternoon. Relax and enjoy the "disco". D☺

Errrmmm I'm still a nutter been up since six and done all my washing!!! So what's all this shopping in the morning then shopping in the afternoon!!! Anyone would think you like it!!☺

Hey, he was in a chatty, upbeat mood. Demi enjoyed these moments of banter and couldn't resist pulling his leg with a play on his use of words.

I've heard of a butter bean. A nutter been is a new one on me.☺ Shopping – its good exercise – that's my excuse anyway. ☺ D

Demi enjoyed the fun and it was lovely to be so chatty, even if it was only texting. At moments like these it felt like they were right next to each other. Their compatibility coming through in the humour and trust that was hidden within the words. Was she fantasising or was there more to it? Can you really fall in love through texting?

Then, there were no more texts and no texts for the rest of the day. Demi knew he was obviously busy shopping with his daughter and she understood that. She herself was busy. It was just that she missed him. Still being determined to only text in reply and not to keep taking the lead Demi resisted texting that evening to ask how his day had gone. Keeping her resolve was the only way Demi would be able to tell whether he was really interested or whether he was just being kind.

Despite her good intentions the day before, Demi had woken Sunday morning disappointed that she still had not had a reply. So what if he had a 'girlfriend'! So what if they had spent the night together and were having a cosy Sunday morning! What about me? She thought selfishly. Next time she'll be stronger – maybe! She couldn't help herself today – in for a penny, in for a pound!!

Hey how was your disco shop yesterday? My 2 trips were great fun. Hope you've got more exciting plans than me for today – housework, paperwork & Ironing!! Have fun! D☺

Now what? How long would she have to wait this time? In the meantime she decided to be true to her text and busy herself with the housework. After several agonising hours, with the constant checking of her phone, finally it went 'ping'.

Hi u – sounds like you've had a rocking weekend!!! Thought I'd done all my chores yesterday – washed cars, washing, ironing then went out for a pizza with the lady I've been dating but it didn't quite go to plan! Anyway thought I could flake out with the tabloids on the settee this afternoon but nothing in the fridge and my daughter hasn't done the cleaning as promised!! Ever feel life's not going to plan!!☺

At last! A mention of the 'lady' and topping that, a not very flattering one. There was hope after all. His day was clearly not going quite to plan and Demi felt he needed a bit of cheering up. She decided to reply with some casual friendliness and optimism and not to keep him waiting too long.

That's life.....& children!☺ Have tackled the housework & now need to decide which of the other 2 exciting tasks to do next. Thought I'd have coffee & toast while I weigh up my options!! Sounds like you've got an exciting choice between Tesco or takeaway – choose wisely!!☺

He was obviously at a loose end as it wasn't long before her phone 'pinged' again.

Hey u I'll have you know that I've been to Waitrose!!!! Only because I've got the patience of a Gnat and love using the self-scanner.... Boys with toys ehh!!!☺

This time she thought she would leave it a bit longer before replying so that she could savour the moment for longer. She also wanted to let her imagination tell the story of the sorry date and how it hadn't gone to plan. She liked it when the ball was in her court. It took the pressure off, in some way. Although choosing the right words to respond brought their own set of challenges. In the end she opted for a short reply using the class differential he had introduced as the basis for the banter.

Hey, hark at you – uptown boy! Welcome to my downtown world!!☺

He must have enjoyed that because, almost in record time, he replied.

Hey you'll always be Chrissy Brinkley in my eyes!!☺

This sent Demi into a tizzy. Who was Chrissy Brinkley? She needed to know this before she could even think about replying. Was he being rude? Funny? Suggestive? She had no idea, but she did know someone who would. Jenny, she would know who Chrissy Brinkley was and she would know just what to say too.

Straight away Demi sent a text to Jenny in South Africa. At times like these the miles didn't matter, although it would be lovely if they weren't there at all. She simply asked Jenny "Who is Chrissy Brinkley"? The message came back "A beautiful model who was married to Billy Joel – why do you want to know"?

Now Demi understood the context and was shocked. Did Josh really mean what he had put in his text or was he playing? Without asking him outright she would never know the real answer. Anyway, how would he know what Demi looked like, he hadn't seen her properly for years.

How could she explain her need to know who Chrissy Brinkley was via text to Jenny? She decided to ask Jenny if she was available to Skype. That way she could explain all the gory details and share the recent texts. After all she had been keeping Jenny updated on the whole texting affair so she was up to speed with recent events.

Demi had explained the text that she had sent to Josh when she had referred to 'Uptown Boy' and 'Downtown World'. As it all fell into place Jenny realised where the reference to Chrissy Brinkley had come from and told Demi that she should be very flattered. Jenny then helped construct a suitable response. And, eventually, a couple of hours later she went back with:

Thank you – I'm very flattered! Well that's the ironing done – phew! The paperwork can wait till tomorrow, which will mean another early start. Ce la vie!! D☺

Demi couldn't help wondering what had happened with his lady friend. Was she still on the scene? If not, perhaps a mention in her next text of meeting for coffee or a drink might be appropriate. Would Josh ask her or would she have to make the first move – again!? Maybe she should back off and give the nonchalant, Lasse fair attitude. That alternative therapy was supposed to work wonders. Or at least it did in the books and films!

The next week crept by with Demi determined to wait for him to reply. She needed to know whether he was thinking about her like she was thinking about him.

CHAPTER EIGHT
Josh, Josh, Josh

S HE WAS DRIVING home from work on Friday evening. It was cold and dark with the clocks due to change that weekend. Stuck in traffic with her mind on the rain that was persistently covering her windscreen and distorting her vision, her phone 'pinged' making her jump and bringing her back to reality. Desperate to see who it was from and conscious that she shouldn't look while driving she was suddenly keen to get home. What was it with this traffic? Didn't these people have homes to go to?

As soon as she pulled into her parking lot and turned the engine off she grabbed her phone. Yes, it was from Josh. Demi had held her resolve and had waited the whole week for this.

Hiya how was your week? Mine flew by – mind you I've been on holiday for the last two days – looking at emails every 5 minutes & stacks of Board papers (in every sense!) for the weekend!! I'm a busy boy tonight (yes me!!) Got a secondary school reunion in Southbourne in a minute then hacking it over to town (alias cattle market) for a grammar school reunion!! If you're out remember to repeat Josh....Josh....Josh... Before you ask I did spend the afternoon doing my ironing!!☺

Wow, that was interesting, a local boy, she hadn't expected that. And he went to a local school that was a rival school to hers. They were always in competition. She wondered how old he was and whether they might have met or gone to any of the same places at the same time back then. The reference to the grammar school as well meant that he must have gone there for 6th form and A levels. She wondered then whether he had gone to University. She remembered reading on 'google' that he had married in his early 20's so he may not have done the Uni thing.

She went into her apartment, unpacked her things and changed into track pants and tee shirt. After pouring a well-earned glass of wine she focused on her reply.

Busy week with lots of interesting union activity – looking forward to a weekend of Board papers too! Lucky you having 2 days off – hope you made time for fun in between the emails. Local school boy eh? Surprised you admitted to that!! I was supposed to be out with the girls from work tonight only cancelled last minute as I've worked them too hard and they're knackered – what is it with youngsters of today? Careful who you s'moo'ch with tonight udderwise you could end up milking it! ☺ Glad to hear you've done the ironing – well done! Have fun. D☺

Demi was using his reference to a cattle market as the source of her humour and told herself not to expect a reply that night as he was out, having fun, she hoped.

She was however disappointed when she had not had a reply by Saturday lunchtime and still being determined to let him reply she busied herself by thinking of excuses for him. After all, if he had been out with the lads and had a good time then he probably had a hangover. He may have taken his hangover to the gym or he may have gone out with his daughter. Or worse! He may be out with his 'lady'. She didn't like that thought, she preferred her stories from earlier in the week about the lady friend no longer being around and decided to stick with these images.

Letting other things distract her Demi buried herself in her usual routine of housework and shopping. Before she knew it she was back into the ritual of Saturday night TV for company and entertainment.

As she nestled down on the sofa her phone 'pinged'. Excitedly she picked it up and disappointedly saw that it wasn't from Josh. Her disappointment didn't last long though as it was a message from her friend, Sarah.

Sarah was at a loose end and was inviting Demi out for a drink at a local trendy bar. Demi could easily have declined having resigned herself to a Saturday night in front of the TV. Instead she throw caution to the wind and replied with an upbeat 'yes' before she changed her mind.

Quickly running in to the bedroom and bathroom she was ready within ½ hour, in a taxi and arriving at the bar at the same time as Sarah.

She even managed to find a few minutes to quickly send a text to Josh (despite withholding all day and going back on her self-made promise) to let him know her good fortune. Keeping it quick and light and remembering to bring in a link to his previous text she went for:

My turn to go out tonight. Was just about to get ready for bed when got invited out!☺ Don't worry – will remember to repeat Josh...Josh.... Josh. D☺

She didn't have to wait long for a reply – maybe he was jealous after all? Just as she and Sarah were relaxing and chatting over their first drink she heard her phone 'ping'. Smiling inwardly, she knew instinctively that it was from him, she pulled her phone out of her bag and read:

Hey you wild thing you!! So where are you off to you women of the moment ... I've been Tesco shopping with my daughter tonight... Man of the people me (after you ribbed me about Waitrose!!) Was thinking either to shake a leg and go to the local pub (only 200 yards away) or pig out on cornetto's with that DVD Inception... If you can explain to me what it's all about I'd be ever so impressed!!!☺

She decided he could wait until the morning before replying; one, because she wanted to make him wait and two, because she needed to concentrate on a reply and she couldn't do that, drink and hold a conversation with Sarah at the same time. Also, there was a rather nice group of men on another table that she and Sarah were enjoying flirting with! Never being ones to miss an opportunity!!

Demi had a really lovely evening. Sarah was always good fun to be with and last night had been no exception. They had left the bar quite late as they had joined the group of lads and had great fun making new friend and having a really good time.

The next morning Demi was up early and decided to make it her second mission (first mission being coffee!) to compose a reply to Josh. After several attempts, slightly hindered by the alcohol from the night before, she settled for:

Testing out the downtown world hey? Was it miraculous or was that just the inception?☺ Thought I'd take the hangover to the gym. Then popping to downtown Tesco before heading home to tackle Board papers and ...you guessed it...the ironing!! No weekend is complete without a bit of ironing!☺

Clearly she had no idea what film Josh had been referring to or who was starring in it. Having sent the text she decided she would go to the gym as she had told him, as it would stop her from phone watching and distract her for an hour or so.

As it was, he replied quite quickly, which Demi didn't see until much later due to the gym and Tesco shop.

Hey lightweight just because you were out painting the town red last night... Saddo here was at the gym at 7.30...remember how competitive I am to win that "no life" award!!! I know why they are called Board papers... Ended up watching the Hurt Locker with my daughter last night which was nice! Have a good time at Tesco's...I've even got my own club card... Boy this new divorced life is not as I imagined!!☺

She enjoyed reading this text. It was fun and also told her some more about his life. He was obviously close to his daughter and still hurting from the pain of splitting with his wife.

As soon as she got back home Demi settled down to composing her reply. Keeping it succinct she managed to let him know about her pending trip and to put in some flirting.

Ok so you win again, although I must be a close second if not a joint first! As you can probably tell I am not a movie buff. Don't knock Tesco club card – it's just about to pay for me to go to South Africa for the month in February and I've already started packing!!☺☺ Whilst divorced life can have its lonely moments it can also have its fun ones too. When else would you get away with texting someone like me? D☺

Well, that obviously did the trick!! Not! Unless Demi had really wanted to scare him off. When she hadn't received a reply by the end of Monday, she knew she would have to wait until at least Friday before she would hear from him again. That's if he hadn't been put off by her up front approach.

Several times throughout the week Demi read and re-read her last text to Josh to see if she could fathom what could have really frightened him off. She decided that if he had been scared off by that then there really wasn't any hope of their relationship (if that's what it was called) going any further.

She resigned herself to not hearing from Josh again as she was definitely determined not to send another text. Feeling a bit sad she was also cross with Josh for being so weak.

CHAPTER NINE
Love Handles

THERE WAS NO-ONE more surprised than Demi when her phone 'pinged' with a message on Friday evening and it was from Josh. She had taken the week convincing herself that it was over, that she had scared him off and wouldn't hear from him again.

Hi how's your week gone?? I've been interviewing for a solicitor all week forgot how boring a breed they are! I get bored so easily so I try to play up but my HR lady won't let me!! She does treat me with sweets if I'm good for the whole hour though!! Tell me that you'd let me muck around if we were recruiting again!! Off with my adopted family for an Italian tonight. Boy having 4 adopted kids is sure expensive on the pocket money front!!☺

It was as if all Demi's emotional self-talk from the week evaporated in an instant. He had obviously been thinking about her all week too. Why else would he be reminiscing in his text and recalling the time, several years ago, when they had worked together?

She was a little concerned however of the mention of his 'adopted family' and four adopted kids and wondered how these featured in his life and where they were from. Her first thought was that they belonged to his lady friend and he was already settling into being a father figure. Pushing this thought aside, she decided it better to make light of it. She went with a chatty reply adding in her weekend plans.

Had fat grumpy NEDs eating out the palm of my hand. They knew I was good, now they know I'm blooming good!!☺ Sounds like your HR lady has got you sussed! And just as well we're not recruiting again as I don't see the point of it if it can't be fun so who knows what we'd end up with!! Make sure you go gentle on him – the Italian that is!☺ How many kids? Oh well, it's only money! Have fun. Carving pumpkins tomorrow with my nieces (17 & 20!) and then having a Halloween tea party – they want me to dress up! Help!! D☺

By Sunday morning Demi was both disappointed and surprised not to have received a reply. This only deepened her suspicion that he had been out with the 'lady' and her four kids, had stayed the night and was spending the weekend with them. He therefore wouldn't be thinking of Demi. Was he using her? Were they ever going to be anything other than text friends, as, let's face it; they didn't really know each other, did they? How could they? They hadn't met or spoken face to face for ten years, unless a brief encounter in a coffee shop more than two years ago counts!?

Being 'testy' she decided to interrupt his love affair to see if she could spark a response during his love nest weekend, as she had developed the situation to be. As she sent another text she wondered whether he might actually be at the gym or out running. If he was still in bed, with her, then so be it. If her text sparked a jealous conversation between the two 'lovers', that would be a result.

Hey u. Hope you had fun with the Italian and 4 children.☺ Thanks for your help yesterday as whatever you did worked as I got away without dressing up!☺ Just off to the gym. No doubt you're already back and tucking into bacon butties.☺ Have a good day. D

His reply, which she didn't have to wait too long for, surprised her and made her feel very guilty for having jumped to such jealous conclusions. Served her right, she self-chastised, for being so nasty, which wasn't usually like her.

Hiya, you so know me – yes I've already been for a very wet run. Found some handles on my sides so guess I must be putting on weight after the first round of the divorce! So back out there pounding the streets! Glad your "gig" went well last night – I've been a bit of a miserable git all weekend as up much of the night doing my divorce finances for court week after next! Off to my mums now to type it all up... It's like returning to the womb!☺

Although Josh's text was a fairly quick reply Demi didn't see it until later as she was in the gym. If she had seen it before going to the gym she would have been worrying about it and not able to concentrate. She would also have been frustrated at not being able to reply. Now, sitting with a coffee, Demi could read it carefully and think about the right words to use.

Having wrapped herself in guilt for her suspicious and nasty thoughts of the previous day, Demi felt obliged to make amends in her reply. She therefore went out of her way to be helpful, friendly and a little flirty.

That's what mums are for & we wouldn't have it any other way. Our baby boys are very special! Seriously – it sounds like a horrible time for you. If there is anything I can do to help please ask. I can type, have a computer and have excellent listening skills. All with no strings. Feel free to take advantage of this once in a lifetime offer!☺ Commonly known as "love" handles.☺ You might want to keep them as you never know when they might come in handy!!☺

His reply, which followed a short while later, was a good attempt on his part to keep cheerful in what must be a very dark place for him. He also made Demi laugh out loud and maybe fall, just a little bit more, in love with him. Oh, if only she could be there to help him through this.

Thanks.☺ You're right the love handles have saved me before... When I was in the loft and stepped between the rafters it was only the love handles that wedged me between the rafters of my daughter's bedroom as my feet dangled!! I'm trying the final cheer up solution... Shopping with my daughter in town!!☺

Demi decided not to keep him waiting and to keep up the light heartedness in the hope of helping him to keep his spirits up.

Haha! Wish I could have witnessed that!!☺ There's nothing like a bit of retail therapy – And I should know!! PS – I'm beginning to notice that you might actually do more shopping than me – and that takes some beating!!☺ Have fun. D☺

Clearly keeping with the jovial mood his reply was also quick and again made Demi laugh.

Opps rumbled! I'm Josh.....And I think I may have a shopping addiction!!!☺☺☺

This time Demi thought best to give him space for the rest of the day. His reply didn't need an immediate response so she decided to wait until the morning so that she could start the week off with him and wish him well. She also wanted him to know that she would be in London, in case he was as well.

Hi u shopaholic! Hope you've had a good start to your week. I've been allowed out today! I'm on the 7.59 to the big city (earliest cheap cattle class ticket – perks of the NHS!) Have a good rest of the week. D☺

Little did she anticipate the fun banter that was to follow. She really was falling for this guy and her desire to meet up, even just for coffee, was beginning to burn deeply.

Hey you lightweight! I was at canary wharf at 7.45 this morning!! Hope you've brought your coat!! Having lunch with the IBSA Board! What train are you catching on the way back?☺

Might have known you'd get there first!☺ The NHS can't stretch to that expensive time of day! My meeting is due to finish around 4 so hope to get the 5-ish train back. What time are you heading back? Enjoy your lunch!☺

Lunch with the IBSA Board and enjoyable don't go together!! I think of it like jury service... Keep my head down until they remember I haven't been for a while!!! I'm on the 2.35/3.05 (does the fact I know these times make me a train spotter!!??) As I've got to get back to the office as out again tomorrow to Ipswich!! Boy I get all the glamour sites!!☺

From shopaholic to "anorak" in the space of a few minutes! Your credibility rating could just have taken a nose dive!☺ Ipswich? There must be something glam about it somewhere? Maybe that's your task for tomorrow to find something good, fun or glam about it & report back.☺

Will do boss!!☺

Oh my, that was so close to a meet up chance! With just a hint of doubt Demi wondered whether he really meant to meet up if the times had worked or whether they were useful as a good excuse to making an offer that he could then get out of by using the times to his advantage.

On second thoughts, being male he probably wasn't that clever at being that devious. That was something us women were usually best at, which is why we thought these suspicious things in the first place.

Even though it was technically Demi's turn to reply she wanted to hold off for as long as possible. She wondered whether Josh would follow through on the Ipswich joke or whether his week would consume him. Demi was out on the Friday night to a friend's firework party with it being the day before Bonfire Night and had very little time to think about sending a text to Josh. She was also staying overnight and didn't get any time alone to text.

With the relationship moving into a bit of a pattern Demi had hoped Josh would text on Friday night and was a little surprised when she didn't receive his next text until Saturday evening. She was however concerned at the tone of his text and felt some of his anguish for the events to come.

Hi u how's tricks?? Hopefully not burning anything down tonight? If you are can you please put my "ex" matrimonial home to the top of the list! Got court on

Wednesday so really not looking forward to this week! Got a load of young girls in my lounge watching movies for a sleepover (sounds racy but some days my daughter and her friends takeover!!) So up again for the sad git Saturday night awards and off to the gym to make myself scarce!! Have I done enough to win??☺

After a long pause and a lot of thought Demi hoped her reply contained a level of empathy, support and light hearted flirting to help lift his mood a little.

Almost. I've been DIY shopping and made a start on some jobs. Going to walk to the local sports ground to watch the fireworks with Aaron & Nadia (eldest & fiancée). That's my exercise for today as it's a good couple of miles or so.☺ *Feel free to join us if you like. Will hit the gym 1st thing. Have a fashion show to do in the week so need to tone a few bits!!*☺ *Have fun. D*☺

At least the rejection that followed was kind and hidden within a context of flirting, emotion and kindness.

Blimmy you and your fashion shows it's like texting Kate Moss!! DIY ehh I'm impressed, that really is likely to win the sad prize!! It's kind of you to offer for me to join you I'd love to another time – I'm doing something I don't often do..... Feeling sorry for myself with the court case this week.... Definitely a single person sport!! Off to help some friends buy a car at 7am (thought I'd clarify that!) so I'll be checking up on you gyming "first thing" now!! Have a good evening.☺

Already off on her walk to the sports ground with Aaron and Nadia to watch the fireworks Demi didn't get chance to read Josh's text until she was sat in a local bar close to the bonfire night venue.

Although Josh's text left Demi feeling a little sad, more for what Josh was personally suffering rather than for the let down on the date invite, she replied with a light hearted update.

DIY queen me. Another one to add to the list!!☺ Too much self-indulgence isn't good for you – what happened to the retail therapy? Oh! What happened to the report on Ipswich? Surely it wasn't that dull otherwise it would be called Dulwich.☺ Decided to go via the pub for a "swift half" before freezing our wotzits over at the sports ground! Enjoy the car viewing. D☺

Demi didn't expect a reply and concentrated on enjoying her evening. When she got home she noticed she had a text message and was surprised to see that it was from Josh, especially after his earlier text. He was obviously bored! And thinking of her.

So how were the fireworks then.?? At my desk working on a Saturday night!! Wish those blooming fireworks would keep the noise down!! Reckon freezing bits off is a close second!!!☺

Demi decided that she would reply, even though it was late, in case he was still at work and if so she wanted to bring him some light relief. If he was already back home and in bed then she would be pleased.

They were really good thanks. I even went on a fun fair ride & screamed loads! You should try it sometime, its good stress relief!!☺ Working on a Saturday night – you are a nightmare!! From anorak to scrooge or should I just put you down as a grumpy old git?☺ Go on - smile - it won't hurt you.☺☺ Just got home & place looks like a bomb's hit it. No.2 son has obviously been home & gone out again!! Oh well tidying will soon warm me up!

Demi was very surprised to receive a reply so quickly.

Blimmy sounds like you had a right rave!! Hey by the sounds of it if anyone needed an anorak it's not me! Yes I did smile thanks first time in a while! Enjoy the gym in the morning.☺

That was a lovely note to go to bed on. She knew she had fallen asleep smiling as her dreams were full of Josh and the wonderful times they were spending together, the things they should be doing together, and would be if Demi got her way.

When Demi woke the next morning she found that she was still smiling. Jumping out of bed she got ready and headed straight for the gym. Josh had promised to check up on her and she didn't want to disappoint.

The one thing keeping her going at the gym was the hope of receiving the 'promised' text by the time she had finished. When she got back to the changing rooms she decided to keep her anticipation and not look at her phone until she had showered, dressed and was sat in the coffee shop.

It was 11 o'clock when she arrived back home, disappointed and flat, as no text from Josh had emerged. In her usual way she had rationalised it as after all he was travelling and with friends and was probably caught up in everything with no time to think of her. Eventually she decided to text him, to jolt his memory and remind him of her existence. After all he could choose whether he wanted to reply or not, couldn't he?

Hey how was the car viewing? What make, model, engine size – and more importantly what colour?!☺

Surprisingly she didn't have to wait long for his reply.

Still on location in Surrey!! All the way to look at a VW caravel (van with seats in my book!!!)....My friends have hundreds of kids...and aren't even Catholics!!!☺

And she was even quicker, again! My! She really must learn to slow it down a bit!!

I hope you've got your warm "anorak" with you as it's blooming chilly out there today!!☺ *Just about to dust down the CV as seen a job that's worth applying for. Keep warm & have fun! D*☺

Hey I'm into parkas!!☺

Wanting to keep the fun going, at least in her head, Demi managed to delay her reply for a while.

I hope it's got a furry edged hood!!☺

And that was it. Silence. She already knew that on Wednesday morning, the day Josh had mentioned he was due in court, she would send him a good luck text. She would do this regardless of whether he replied to her last text or not. She could sense that he was worried about the situation and he obviously had to put it before anything else.

Having this knowledge helped Demi to understand why she hadn't received a response and all was quiet from Josh. She was pleased she had given him the space.

CHAPTER TEN
Ecstasy and Despair

O N WEDNESDAY morning, as premised to herself, Demi sent Josh a quick text.

Hi. Just a note to say, hope all goes well today. Take care. D

She wouldn't have worried if he hadn't replied as she hadn't really expected him too. She only wanted him to know she was thinking of him. However, that didn't stop her from being over excited when her phone 'pinged' almost straight away.

Thanks, it's really kind of you to remember.☺

This made her heart melt. She wondered how many other people had remembered and what support he had. She wished so much that he had let her in more and that she could physically be there with him to offer and give her support. She could feel inside that this was going to be a difficult day for him.

She wondered when and if she would hear from him again as she didn't want to chase him to find out how it had gone. It wasn't her place and somehow it would seem intrusive for her to ask him.

Demi had just climbed into bed on Friday night, bored from yet another evening in front of the TV, when her phone 'pinged'. Not sure what to expect at this late hour she tentatively picked up the handset.

Hiya how's your week gone? Mine was a hoot! Divorce court was a bit like a wedding only in reverse! Instead of everyone lining up as you left the church and throwing confetti my 'ex' wife's family all lined up outside the court so that I had to walk through their cordon to get in whilst they gave me, as my kids say 'evils'!! Off to Cannock at 5am tomorrow to look at another car for my soon to be 'ex' friends if I keep having to do this early weekend 'gig'!! Have you got a fun packed weekend planned??☺

She was horrified at the content of his text. What a terrible ordeal to have had to have gone through. She was at least heartened by the last part of the message, which was a bit lighter hearted and showed that he had friends around him that Demi found comforting.

Demi decided to wait until the morning to reply. That way she could take all night to compose something suitable.

Saturday morning arrived and Demi was ready to send her reply.

Wednesday sounds like it was a horrible time – at least you have got through it now – well done!☺ Whatever I do this weekend is going to be more exciting than a 5am start to look at child friendly cars!! Now, make it convertible with 2 seats & I'll be there in a flash!!☺ I'm off to town for some Xmas shopping today ☺ ☺ & must finish my application for a new job tomorrow (I'm struggling with the whole 'sale yourself' bit)!!☹ Hope you've got some good plans for the rest of the weekend. Have fun. D☺

On reflection and particularly after going a couple of hours with no reply, Demi decided that her text had been too open to allow for no response being needed until at least Sunday night or Monday morning. She didn't want to wait that long. What all weekend without 'chatting' to Josh!? So while out shopping and enjoying the sunshine she decided to drop him a quick text.

Hope the weather's good in Cannock cos its fab 'roof down' sunshine here. Definitely no need for an anorak or parka (with or without a furry edged hood)!!☺

By mid-afternoon, just as she was beginning to think the worst, that Josh would never reply, her phone finally 'pinged' with a text from him. Feeling nervous, as she wasn't sure of his mood or whether he was getting fed up with her. She reminded herself that just because she was in love and enjoying their relationship didn't mean that he felt the same way.

Well I'm back from foggy Brum several Costa's later with a black A team van for the family with 4 kids who haven't learnt about contraception yet!! Think I'd rather have been doing Xmas shopping in my parka that's how bad it was!! So what's this job you're going for then??☺

She was excited to hear from him and really pleased that he had asked a question prompting her to reply. She wanted to hold out for as long as she could only she was too excited and so wanted to 'talk' to him. So she set to work to create her response. She was also pleased to finally link up the connection with the 4 children. At least they didn't belong to the 'girlfriend'.

Pleased you're back safely and having had some success. Whoever invented Costa should be made a saint!☺ Job is a 2yr contract for a HRD role at a government funded hospital on a small island in the Pacific!! Just got back from shopping. Why is there never a man around when you need them to carry the bags?! ☺ What have you got planned for the rest of the weekend? D☺

It wasn't long before she received a reply. He was obviously in a 'chatty' mood and managing to maintain some light humour despite the personal issues he was going through.

You jammy so and so, Pacific Island ehhh! Just off to eat the family I've helped out of house and home as a payback for dragging me up to Brum!! Tomorrow back around my Mum's table answering my 'ex' wife's questions on where the missing Libyan millions have gone!! Guess the shopping was a success!☺

She was determined to keep his spirits up and set about creating a witty yet empathetic reply. An hour later, being sure she had the right balance and pleased with the result, she pushed 'send'.

Strawberry is my favourite, followed by blackcurrant (jam that is!). I hope the family that you are just off to eat taste nice!!☺ Ex-wife's ehh! She should have looked after it better!!☺ Shopping was a good start – it's a shame to do it all at once otherwise there is nothing left to do next weekend and the weekend after and the weekend after.............. I'm off to see a show tonight that my sister has produced and half the family are in (they're like that my lot). My contribution is to pay for the tickets and go to watch!! It's a cowboy cabaret so lots of line dancing and hoedown I expect. I'll have to get my "Daisy Duke" shorts and cowboy boots dusted down!!☺ Have fun. D☺

Having convinced herself that he was in a 'chatty' mood she soon became disheartened when she hadn't received a reply after an hour. She was pleased that she was going out that evening as at least she had something to occupy her and help to keep her mind off him, if that was at all possible. Knowing that he was with his friends helped as he would be busy with them and he was with company.

However, Saturday evening came and went and so did Sunday morning. Demi did her best to keep busy and to keep distracted from thinking of Josh. Nothing much was helping. He was consuming every thought and action. Every time she did something or thought something Josh would feature. What would he do or say if he were there doing and thinking with her? Her imagination was letting her include him in everything. Asking herself what would Josh do about this? What would Josh say about that? How would he feel? What would he think? She so wished he were a 'real' part of her life and not just a fantasy. How could she make that happen?

Completely lost and consumed with her fantasy and day dreaming Demi was somewhat surprised to find a text message on her phone that she had missed. Not wanting to believe it would be from Josh she told herself it was from one of her boys, probably asking for food or money!! Bringing herself back to earth she opened the message. And was delighted!

Hiya sorry I'm late replying been camped out at my Mum's doing my marathon response for the divorce – very distraught at missing the Daisy Duke hot pants – would have even been prepared to play the part of Boss Hog to see that!!☺ PS if you don't mind me saying I think they have shoppers addiction clinics that one can go to if one thinks one might have a problem!!☺☺ PPS best of luck for the interview tomorrow but don't wear the bikini it might just show them that you're a bit too keen!!☺

Her reply, well, she thought it was chatty and would generate another text from Josh.

Well done for getting the response done. I think I might write a play specifically with a part of the "boss" for you – it would be fun to see you in a Stetson!!☺ Is that a suggestion that one attends an addiction clinic that one visits already?!☺ It's just the application that needs to be in tomorrow. I'm still a long way off interview stage!! Thankfully all done.☺ Now have just embarked on that wonderful task that no weekend is complete without doing – ironing!! Doing it while watching last night's Strictly makes it slightly more enjoyable – just!!☺ What have you got planned for the week ahead?

This time Demi remembered to ask a question at the end in the hope of prompting a response. Clearly though, Josh was otherwise engaged. Demi's emotions were being stretched all over the place. From being in love and having Josh with her, even if only in her head, to them splitting up and never having the chance to meet. Taking her from ecstasy one minute to complete despair the next.

However, her anguish continued for the whole week. It was Friday before she heard anything from him. She had been determined not to text again. She really did need to prove to herself that it wasn't her doing all the running and that Josh was at least keen to keep a 'friendship' with her.

She had already been wondering whether she should text Friday evening if she hadn't heard from him. So she was pleased when the decision making was taken from her and his text unexpectedly arrived at lunchtime.

CHAPTER ELEVEN
Friends

*S*O HOW'S YOUR *week been? Got a fun packed weekend lined up? I've one last challenge left.... To stay awake at a National Bank presentation over lunch!! Not hard I hear you say....But I was the fool who got up to do all his washing at 5am this morning and did a supermarket sweep in 15 mins round Sainsbury's a moment ago.....OCD maybe??? Perhaps what with you working in the NHS you know of a cure?☺*

It took a strong coffee and a long admin break for Demi to compose her response. Being brave she included a flirty innuendo in the hope of it being taken up and immediately visualised the amazingly wonderful time they were about to have.

Hi. My week has been very busy and if you know anyone who can magic a couple of extra days without telling anyone else they'll be my hero!! 24hrs 7 days is just not enough! Two more meetings then a stack of admin before I can escape to a weekend of shopping!! Got to feed my addiction somehow!☺ I would say you're a sensible fool getting your chores done early.☺ I've had too many early mornings and late nights working to have done mine so will need to fit it in around the shopping! The best cure for OCD is TLC and a glass of bubbly and I know a good NHS provider for this.☺☺ What are your plans for the weekend? How's your week been? What addictions will you be feeding?☺☺

Bringing herself back to earth she remembered, that as far as she knew, there was still a 'lady' friend in the mix. Demi really must find a way to bring her back into the 'conversation' and find out how 'real' she really was. And Josh's next text gave her the perfect opportunity.

Hiya. Glass of wine and TLC sound a great tonic!! J☺

Forgot to mention that this requires a minimum of 2 so make sure you ask your lady to share with you and enjoy the moment!! Have fun. D☺

Wow! She was impressed with her response and hoped that Josh's reply would give her the answer she was prompting. How long would she have to wait? The anticipation and excitement already becoming intense, she went straight off in search of a good diversion for an hour or so. Thankfully he didn't make her wait too long.

That's a long sad story only on a par with Bambi!!!☺

She couldn't help the huge grin that spread across her face and the wonderful warm feeling pulsing through her whole body. This was perfect. Obviously she couldn't tell Josh how pleased she was with this news. She would have to give her emotions time to calm down before composing a suitably compassionate reply. This proved more difficult than she thought and she couldn't help being pushy and flirtatious as her excitement was still bubbling through and taking over her whole being.

Oh dear! I'm sorry to hear that because I'm afraid that the cure won't work unless it's shared!!☺

She knew exactly the amount of TLC to apply and exactly where she was going to apply it. All she had to do was drive over to his place; pour him a glass of bubbly, fix some dinner and the TLC could begin.

His resistance would be futile as he became a martyr to the cause. The flirty banter between them, the fun in their eyes and the growing inability to hold back from that gaze and desire for those lips. The longing to touch and run fingers through hair. To pull each other close and feel his heart pounding against hers as passion rises from deep inside. As the intensity increases and they both want more of each other, she pulling at this shirt and he running his hands over her body.

*

It was Sunday morning and Demi had heard nothing from him. Was he really that scared and scarred by women?

She wasn't going to give up, especially now that the 'other' woman was off the scene. Filled with renewed confidence and not wanting to miss an opportunity she decided to text again and to include a little teaser about her own feelings to see if he picked up the bait.

Hey u how's your weekend going? I got bored shopping so came home to find Chas wanted to play "my mum's a free taxi driver". He wanted to go into town and then be dropped at the sports ground. So we put the roof down, turned the music up and sang & jigged our way across town – great fun!☺ Off to choose & buy a new floor for my hallway this morning. I've got a man to fit it and I've not chosen it yet!! Then probably should face the Board papers & fit the gym in at some point although my "get up & go" seems to have "got up and gone" this weekend.☹ If you're still needing a cure I still know a good NHS provider.☺ Have fun. D☺

She wasn't expecting his reply and immediately berated herself for her lack of compassion. She had assumed he had been scared off and was sulking rather than hurting and having to cope on his own with a difficult situation. How could she put this right? How could she help him? If only he would let her in.

Hi D... You're such a poser!!! I'm just jealous mind you! Friday night was a disaster my drunken daughter and her friends had a falling out at 3 in the morning... Neighbours, landlords involved ever since... I've been taking it out on my body this morning. Done a gym and a long run already and washed everything in sight. Now off to see an old friend and her kids for some more noise torture... why do I do it!!! Have a great day.☺ J

Because she was out and about and had been in the gym it was a while before Demi saw his text. And another while before she found the words to send. Demi felt awful. All weekend she had been wrapped up in her own feelings and hadn't thought about Josh's once. She should know by now that every time there was a lull in his texts it was because something serious had happened, and this time was no exception. How could she be so callous and uncaring? Why wouldn't he just let her help? She wouldn't let him down.

If you've got it flaunt it!☺ Your daughter makes my 2 boys seem like angels and that takes some doing I can tell you!!☺☺ Sounds like you need a chill pill to go with the TLC & glass of jungle juice. I know where you can get a prescription, even on a Sunday!☺ I hope it's not too torturous at your friend's. At least you'll get some "grown up" company as well. Enjoy! D☺

So, all these subtle mentions of his 'friend', was this another rival Demi needed to be aware of or was she a true friend? Demi decided that as jealousy wasn't her thing she would prefer to view this 'friend' as a good friend who was providing support to Demi's friend where Demi wasn't able to. And for that Demi would be grateful.

All week Demi waited for Josh's reply. Worried about what he was going through and desperately wanting to provide support, even if it was just a listening ear.

In keeping with a pattern that was evolving Demi managed to get through until Friday before expecting and hoping that Josh would text again. Conscious that she was still the one who always seemed to be taking the lead she was again determined to wait to give Josh chance to text her on either Friday evening or Saturday morning, before giving in and taking control.

By late afternoon on Saturday, having used every distracting tool available to her, Demi couldn't wait any longer. This time Demi was worried about Josh. Worried about what he had to deal with on his own and how he was coping. He seemed to be moving from one drama to another and she wanted this to stop for him, just for a while. Feeling guilty and silly for allowing herself to fall in love with text messages Demi felt as though she needed to give him a way out. Maybe, for him, she was in the way and becoming a nuisance.

Hey you! You've gone quiet on me. I hope all is ok with you. If my fun-friendly banter has got too much let me know & I'll disappear quietly. Whatever you're doing make sure you smile.☺ It'll make whatever it is feel a whole lot better.☺☺ Have fun. D☺

The reply was a very long time coming. Demi's thoughts were going all over the place. Was that it? Was it over? Was he well? Was he back with 'her'? Was his daughter playing up? Was he working? Was he ok? How could she help? What could she do? What should she do? Why won't he let her in? Why was she bothered? Ummm....Good question! Why was she bothered??

Because she cared. Through their texts Demi had grown to care and wanted the opportunity for them to meet up, to see whether there was a mutual desire to be friends, or to develop a relationship. Being friends would be enough. Demi could do this via text, only it would be much easier if they could at least meet up once. This would give them both a better foundation for a friendship. How could she make this happen?

He was a hardworking, family loving man, built on similar values as her. He was also tall, dark and handsome with the most amazing eyes. Physically good to look at, fit, energetic, trendy, smart and generally drop dead gorgeous. What more did she need?

All of these thoughts and dreams filled the hours until eventually Demi took herself off to bed. Feeling lonely and sad, warn out from the constant thoughts of Josh dominating her mind and being, Demi was asleep in no time.

Waking early Sunday morning Demi became excited to see that she had received a text in the middle of the night. Was it from Josh?

Hi D – sorry for the radio silence – been a bit of a stressful week – travelled all over the country and been planning for a Board strategy day next week – Meanwhile divorce stuff is full on fraught with some horrible issues! All in all a toxic combination for a bit of a male feel sorry for one self (which incidentally I'm a black belt at!!) Anyway don't think it fair to share my "black dog" sorry for oneself mood with anyone as I'm selfish!! Also was very concerned to see you handing out NHS prescriptions when I know you're in personnel & I didn't want you getting done for practicing without a licence!!☺ So tomorrow as a cure I'm going Xmas shopping with my daughter (ahh!!!) It's enough to drive one to drink!! Looks like I'll need some tips on shopping from you what with you being an expert! Hope your weekend is going well & that Xfactor wasn't too exciting!!☺

Wow! It was a long one. And full of references to bits of conversation that they have had recently showing that he did take it in and did care; filling Demi with mixed emotions and a feeling of really wanting to give him a big hug. She was pleased he was finding a release in shopping as she could sense that he would enjoy this despite his attempt at making it sound like a chore.

She definitely needed coffee to accompany her while she planned her reply. It would need to include an acknowledgement of his mood, some fun and some encouragement. Demi was pleased with the result.

Hi. Good to hear you're trialling some xmas shopping as part of the cure – its renowned for its positive results!☺ And, I just might have 1 or 2 tips up my sleeve!! ☺ Please be assured Mr B that one is well qualified in all areas of one's practice & there is definitely no licence required!!☺☺ Just for the record, I'm not in "personnel" (tea & tissues) I'm in "HR" (strategy) – clearly I'm not sensitive about this!!☺ It does sound like you're having a bit of a rough time right now. I'm sure it won't be long before it all settles down and that "black dog" will be back to being a "cute puppy"!☺ Luckily my Board meetings were last week so just the public sector strike & possible merger talks to look forward to this week!!☺ Then I've got a few days off to go Xmas shopping (off to Bath with sister, niece & cousin on Friday) & to do some DIY. Never a dull moment ehh?!☺ Enjoy your day & treat yourself to something nice too!!☺☺

Writing this text made Demi think. Yes, she did have an exciting few days ahead and it was going to be good spending time with the female side of her family as they were all good friends. Also she couldn't wait to get a quiet moment with Jaini to update her on the latest with Josh. They hadn't had a minute over the last couple of weeks so there was a lot to update her on.

CHAPTER TWELVE
Baby Steps

DEMI HAD JUST booked her flight to South Africa for a month in February and the whole schedule needed planning. Jenny in South Africa was busy booking adventures and planning the itinerary. It was really going to be a fun trip doing and experiencing a lot of things they hadn't done before. Not that Demi knew what all this would be yet.

Before that though there was Christmas, Demi's favourite time of year, to look forward to; Christmas shopping to do and a new floor to be fitted. Having busied herself with chores and thoughts, she hadn't realised the time, when she heard her phone peep with a new text.

Hey u I'm holding you responsible for leading me astray!! I'm up to 2 jumpers for myself already and I fancy some All Saints boots!! Must start buying the kids presents sometime soon..........

Demi filled with warmth as she read this. He was definitely in a better mood and sounded as if he was really enjoying himself. She really must get in with the Designer labels as he clearly liked a logo or two. Demi thought that she would keep the mood light by returning quickly with a short 'well done' type of text.

Good for you!☺ I except full responsibility & am guilty as charged!! Keep going – you're doing well & there's always next weekend to shop for the kids!!☺

Within no time Josh replied and made her laugh. She couldn't resist her response while still laughing. This would keep her smiling all day.

Phew I feel vindicated!!! Maybe I'll get kids socks!!!☺

Why? Have you got small feet?☺☺

That was it though. No more texts that day. This time Demi was definitely going to wait for him to text first. She felt sure she would have to wait until at least Friday evening, and if not, Saturday sometime so she pitched in for the long haul.

*

Thursday evening and Demi had just settled into a glass of wine and trash TV when she received a text. Assuming it was from anyone other than Josh she lazily reached for her phone and then jumped with delight when she realised that it was from him. Had he got his days muddled?

Hi you how's HR (strategy!!) been this week? Saddo here on my tod. Just at the Duran Duran concert waiting for it to start! When I bought the last ticket a few months ago I was warned it had restricted viewing... What they didn't tell me was that the seat was so far back it's in Hampshire!! Anyway a lot has changed since I last saw this lot....All the guys are bald and the Duran Duran groupies have turned to 20 stone muffin tops!!! No wonder the NHS has its work cut out!!!☺

Although his text made her smile as he was clearly keeping himself cheery Demi couldn't help feeling a bit sad too. She would have done anything to be with him, to keep him company. It didn't seem fair that he was there on his own and she was sat at home bored and alone. How could she get them to meet, just once, as that would be all that they would need?

Hey. Now you really are showing your age!☺ Is it the seat or your eyesight?? Make sure you sing a long at the top of your voice & have fun.☺ My week has been good especially as I am on leave now until next Thursday.☺☺ How did your strategy Board day go? D☺

Demi thought that if she told him she was off for a few days and at a loose end he might take the hint. Anyhow she enjoyed his company through the texts and she would rather have that than nothing.

She enjoyed their quick banter too when it happened and was even more excited when he replied within a few minutes, like he did now.

Hey the support act that are presently on are called "cock & bull"!! I'm not doing anything along with them least it be misinterpreted!!☺ Board strategy went well thanks. So what are you doing on your holiday then??? And don't you say shopping now!!!☺

Was that a leading question? Was he fishing to see if Demi had any 'free' time while she was on leave? In her reply Demi wanted him to get a sense of her having things to do with a balance of also having time to fit more in if offers, such as coffee or a drink, for example, were made.

I hope they don't sound like their name! And....guess what?? I am going shopping – well tomorrow at least! As off to Bath with the girlies for a bit of xmas indulgence.☺☺ Rest of the time will be interspersed with some decorating.☹☹ Also going to another cowboy show so shorts & boots will get another airing!!☺☺ Say "hi" to Monsieur le Bon for me.☺

And then it went quiet, again. How long would she have to wait this time? How long could she wait? Every time she started to enjoy his company and feel part of him it stopped and left her feeling empty and deflated.

Friday was a busy day driving to Bath with her sister and nieces, meeting her cousin and goddaughter and Christmas shopping before driving back. All day Demi had been constantly checking her phone in the hope of a text. He could have at least wished her a fun day. Then maybe he was busy, after all he was a high flyer with a very high profile job.

When Demi had dropped everyone off, unloaded the car and poured a glass of wine she couldn't settle until she sent him a text. Just a short one to check how the concert had gone. Surely that would be ok?

Hi. How was your concert? Did u remember the words or has age really kicked in.?!☺ What have you got planned for the weekend? Don't say shopping cos you'll make me jealous!!☺

This time, having to wait over night before receiving a reply left her worrying again about what Josh might be enduring on his own. Demi decided to get up early and hit the gym. She couldn't face hanging around waiting for a reply, she needed distraction. It wasn't until Demi had showered and was sat in the café with coffee that she realised she had received a reply. Demi was both delighted and relieved.

Hi u they were fab and I hummed and howled with the best of the nutters!!! Mind you couldn't bring myself to hold my phone up in the air!! Went to my adopted family's kid's fete last night...Rave!! Round my mums on solicitors replies today and probably "saddo" gym tonight!! Just focusing on January and then new me will be out starting a new more exciting life!! Now as for that shopping....☺

Despite the pain he was obviously going through Josh was doing his best to keep chirpy. Oh how she wanted to help him. The mention of his mum and the information he provided on his divorce meant that he trusted her with this insight into his life and challenges. Demi felt pleased, warm and wanting even more to find a way to get closer, quicker. These baby steps, chipping away at his strong body armour just wasn't cracking it quickly enough for Demi.

Thinking carefully and planning her reply filled her focus while drinking her coffee. She decided to wait until she got back home before she sent it. She was already conscious that she was smiling like a Cheshire cat and getting some strange looks. She couldn't help it. This is how Josh made her feel, warm, bubbly and full of over brimming smiles.

Morning!! I managed to shift my lazy butt and have done the gym thing this morning!! Plan is to have a 'saddo' quiet night in (Strictly, X Factor, Jungle) and head to the gym early again tomorrow!! – We'll see??!!☺ Get your replies sorted and keep your focus – January sounds like a great goal and fits nicely for a New Year = New You (what a strap line – maybe I should be in Marketing!!) What shopping? I'm jealous already.☹ D☺

She was pleased with this reply and it kept her happy as she got stuck back into her DIY painting. There was still a lot to do before the man arrived to lay her new floor on Monday morning.

Luckily, knowing that Josh was busy writing letters meant that Demi wasn't expecting a reply any time soon. And it was over 24 hours before the excitement returned. Demi filled the time with decorating and Chas had offered to help. They worked hard together and made it enjoyable having music playing, plenty of chat and making excuses for several food and drink breaks.

Hi how's the weekend going Ms HR (Strategy)! Summoned up enough courage to go local Xmas shopping yesterday. Went around the multi-storey once couldn't be bothered so drove straight out again!! It's looking like Christmas Eve after all.... At least I will have to be focused!! Was meant to go to the Outlet Shopping Village this morning (which I don't mind as I always end up with a pair of Diesel jeans for myself!!) But my 4.10am daughter isn't up yet!! Ahh the young today!! Met an old school friend down town last night for a drink which made a nice change! So now I think I'll hit the ironing and Christmas present wrapping as my penance!! Can't wait!! So what's the latest on the Xfactor then??☺

Unfortunately Demi didn't have time to reply as she was out helping at a cowboy show fund raising event. It would be at least 5pm before she got back home. The good thing was it gave her time to think about her reply and as his message filled her with smiles it helped make her afternoon more enjoyable.

When it came to the time for her to reply Demi found she had lots to say and wanted to share with him. She was pleased he had managed to find things to do instead of falling into the woes of his divorce. Demi enjoyed her reply and hoped her question at the end would spark at least one more text from him to keep her going through the week.

I can beat you by an hour with my 5.15am son!! Let's hope for your sake that they weren't together!!! Managed to get a 1ˢᵗ coat of emulsion on my hallway yesterday & thinking about doing a 2ⁿᵈ coat tonight. Then have got 10 doors to gloss. Might decide that the ironing is a more attractive idea instead though!! Just got back from the cowboy show which was fun. What happened to you going to the gym last night then?? I'm pleased you had a good night out instead. I stayed in & did the gym thing again this morning. Think I've earnt myself a glass of wine this evening as a treat!☺ You could watch the Xfactor results show whilst ironing & present wrapping. It's the semi-finals and supposed to be exciting!! Looking forward to 3 days off this week despite all the glossing!! What's your week ahead looking like? D☺

As Demi reflected on her text she became filled with horror. How would Josh interpret her words about her son and his daughter? Would he think she was being critical about his daughter and her behaviour? She felt she needed to put it right straight away and hope she hadn't upset him or he had read too much into it.

Sorry! Just having a texting crisis! I Hope I haven't upset you with my choice of words. What I meant was that my son isn't the sort of chap most Dads would want for their "little girls". He's a bit of a charming womaniser!! Just realised that you might read something different into what I wrote. Sorry. D

Demi was pleased to get a quick reply although nervous about what it might say. Was this too much? Had she overstepped the mark? As she bravely opened and read Josh's reply she felt relieved. He was so lovely she just wanted to melt into his arms and snuggle close.

Hey u nothing to worry about re your son. I didn't give it a moment's thought!! Just preparing a load of paperwork to help someone out with a Cypriot mortgage that they got themselves into... I'm a right sucker for always trying to help someone out!! In freezing London working for the IBSA tomorrow... Yippee last trip to the smog hopefully this year!! Now how's that decorating of your 10 door mansion doing????☺

Ten door mansion! She needed to put him right on this as she hadn't meant to make it sound pretentious. She was keen to reply with something that might engage some banter as being a Sunday night she felt sure it would be next Friday or Saturday before she heard from him again.

Phew!! You would have thought the clue was in the word Cypriot!! The 10 door mansion is a 2 bed flat!! There are lots of cupboard doors!!☺ The glass of wine won in the end & the rest has gone to pot. Never mind – there's always tomorrow!!☺ Enjoy your last trip to the IBSA & make sure you take your anorak!!☺☺

Just as she was giving up hope of a reply she was surprised to hear that familiar 'ping' from her phone.

Hey I'm more of a Barbour guy you cheeky monkey!☺

This made Demi laugh out loud. Josh was obviously feeling relaxed and this made Demi feel close to him. She just knew that together they would have so much fun. She felt a real connection at a sense of humour level and she was sure they would connect on so many other levels as well. Bringing herself back to the moment Demi was eager to respond with a 'one liner' of her own.

I guess if you need a haircut that's the best place to go!! Hee hee☺

And that was it. No more texts that evening and Demi knew she was back in the waiting game. Yes, she understood he was busy and work was his life. She just wanted him to find a bit of time for her, even if just to help break up his day or week. She was at least grateful for his time at the weekends.

CHAPTER THIRTEEN
True Religion

T HE WEEK WAS going to be especially long as Demi had some time off work. Luckily she had plenty to do what with decorating and Christmas shopping. Although all she could think about was how everything she was doing would be different if she was doing it with Josh. What would he think of this? What would he say about that? Where would they go for lunch or coffee? Which shops did he like?

It was Thursday before she knew it and Demi was back at work. If the pattern continued there was only one more day to go. She really hoped that Josh would be first to text on Friday this week as she was beginning to think that it was becoming less one sided and wanted this week to help prove it. Then she would relax and have more faith in his feelings for her.

That evening after a busy day back at work and a busy time over her days off Demi had taken herself to bed early. Just as she was settling down her phone made her jump.

Hi u hope you've had a good week – I thought before you ring the hospitals and Amnesty international I'd let you know that I'm going away this weekend to my sisters!! She has a nice house in the middle of the country in Berkshire with hardly any neighbours – apart from cows... mobile phone signal and most importantly she and her 4 kids are away! So I'm going to chill, read a book and relax!! Can't wait after the week from hell!! Hope you've recovered from all your cowboy stuff last weekend Daisy Duke!!☺

Demi loved the reference to Daisy Duke. More importantly she was inwardly bubbling that he cared enough to let her know he would be away for the weekend.

Demi was also pleased that he was, at last, taking some time out. She only very slightly wondered if he was taking anyone with him and why hadn't he invited her. She replied straight away.

Hey. Sounds fab. Hope you have a wonderful time.☺ Painting just about finished – thank goodness!! Work strange as back to being a 'minion' this week as had to hang up the Director boots again as the 'real' Director is back from mat leave – oh well – it was fun while it lasted!!☺ Busy weekend ahead with painting to finish, panto to see (sister is in it!) & lunch with my Dad on Sunday. Make sure u wrap up warm in your Barbour & I hope you've got matching wellies?!☺ Enjoy conversing with the cows! DD☺

Her DD sign off was reference to her new Daisy Duke name and Demi wondered if Josh would pick up on this.

Demi didn't expect a reply. While she was excited for Josh as he was going away she felt a little lost. Having to face the weekend without any texts from Josh was going to be tough. At least she knew where he was and the reason why there were no texts, which was actually a better situation than normal. Dwelling on that she really hoped he would have a good time and get some rest from the rat race he was in.

It was the morning before Demi saw that Josh had replied. Demi must have fallen into a deep sleep with her thoughts and dreams about Josh.

Boy I'm exhausted hearing about your exploits!! I say let's get someone to knock off the Director so you can takeover!! Glad to see you've got the 10 doors "licked" so to speak – but as for the panto I never had you down as a "they're behind you" kind of girl!!!!! Anyway have a good one.☺

This text would keep Demi going for the weekend. She loved the playfulness and that he was obviously in a relaxed mood. Every time she read and re-read it she felt warm, happy and full of energy. She also knew that she had a permanent grin on her face and her eyes were dancing. This made her whole weekend fun.

As Sunday progressed Demi began to guess that she would have to wait until Friday before the next text arrived. However, this time it was her turn to reply so at least she had a perfectly good reason for texting first when Friday finally arrived. In the meantime Demi resolved to get on with the week, alone and safe in the knowledge that Josh was in a good place and the next move was hers.

Demi was therefore very surprised to find a text on her phone during Sunday afternoon and even more surprised that the text was from Josh. She immediately wondered if anything was wrong.

Hi u what have you been up to this weekend?? Mines been a bit of an adventure – got to my sister's house to find no heating or hot water... I could see me breathe inside!! So I've spent much of the weekend with my bum up against her Aga (have you got the vision?!) reading the economist!!! Went to the local town to do some Xmas present shopping and bought myself a Superdry shirt!!! Did manage to catch up with my American friend on Saturday night who is in the UK for a few days. He has a great sense of humour and always makes me laugh!!☺

Demi smiled at his antics and relaxed. He was fine and appeared to have enjoyed his weekend, despite the cold. She decided to take her time over a reply and sat down to start composing. Demi felt that the time was right to make another attempt at a flirty hint to see if he would take the bait.

Thanks for the vision! I'm glad I've already eaten!!☺ *Sounds like you've had a good time despite the adventure! I hope you've managed to thaw out!*☺ *Have just got back from lunch with Dad. Have finished the painting, put xmas decs up, done a "little" shopping & been to panto – oh no I didn't – oh yes I did!!*☺ *Got present wrapping, ironing & tidying to do – boring! Would prefer a large coffee & walk after the enormous lunch I've just eaten!! Maybe I'll stick some Xmas music on & sing (using the word very loosely!) while I work!*☺ *What's your week ahead looking like? Any xmas parties to go to? D*☺

Using the power of questions to encourage a response seemed to work as it wasn't too long before his reply arrived, just long enough for it to be too dark to go for a walk! Demi wondered if that was his way of being able to ignore her flirty hint as being dark the opportunity for a walk and coffee had been missed. Nevertheless he had replied and the fun, light banter continued.

Boy you lead a charmed life!!! My eldest daughter and I are just putting up a 2 foot pink Xmas tree!! Guess who chose it!!! Got the raving Grants Holding party at the Cumberland on Thursday other than that a mega busy week but at least all local! How about you? ☺

The Cumberland was only up the road from where Demi lived – how could she weave that in to a reply? She was pleased he had a more sensible working week ahead. It was just as well she wasn't with him as she really would need to sort out his Christmas decorations – pink tree!! Really?

The great thing about his text was that he had ended it with asking her a question, which was clearly inviting a response. This was unusual and gave Demi a good sense and feeling of closeness, trust and friendship, which she would take and hang onto for now. Demi went for an upbeat and 'newsy' reply with a bit of flirty fun.

It could be worse – it could be a 6ft pink tree!!☺ I've got 2 Xmas lunches this week & a "black tie" charity do on Wednesday with my modelling chicks. I will then need to be in the gym all weekend to work off the xmas pud & mince pies!! Most exciting of all is my new floor that is getting laid tomorrow – nearly went for a smutty comment & then thought better of it!!☺

It wasn't long before Josh replied. Demi was really enjoying their fun today and her fondness for Josh was definitely growing. She only hoped Josh felt the same. He was difficult to read, especially with only having texts to go by.

Would have preferred the smutty comment!! Boy you know how to live it up with Xmas parties!! I'm feeling like a lightweight!! Got back this morning so went for a long run in the rain to pay ahead for my indulgences this week and make some room for all those puddings!!!☺

As Demi hadn't expected a reply, particularly so quickly, she had busied herself with various chores and had not heard the text come through. She was surprised to find it when she checked her phone a while later. And she loved it! And she loved him!!

Demi decided that her response should include an opportunity for Josh not to reply as she didn't want to become too intense for him. If he wanted to reply he could and Demi would see what the content was as it could be that it would be a good place to leave the weekend banter and to set up the foundation for a new round at the start of the next one.

Planned ahead I see – good move! I might have to resort to getting up extra early & hula hooping with the WII fit!! Always good for a laugh if nothing else!☺ Have fun & don't work too hard – it's Christmas! D☺

There was no reply. That was ok, Demi thought. Let's see how the week goes. She already had her Friday text planned as if she heard nothing from Josh she could text to ask him how his Christmas party had gone. The week had rushed by with all the parties and Christmas excitement. Demi hoped Josh had been having a good week. He had seemed pleased that he was staying local all week and Demi hoped that hadn't changed for him. Demi had managed to wait until the early evening on Friday before texting in the hope that Josh would find time to go first. Not being able to wait any longer Demi hit 'send'.

Hey u. How's your week been? Did u survive your GH "rave" with your integrity intact or are their some good stories to tell? D☺

What Demi hadn't expected was what then followed. Firstly nothing, in terms of a reply from Josh, was forthcoming. Demi knew that if Josh was out on Friday night he may not get chance to reply. She could also excuse a no reply Saturday morning, putting it down to a hangover, out running or time with his daughter.

What Demi hadn't anticipated was having to wait until Saturday evening before receiving anything and being horrified by the content.

Hi Sorry I haven't text (you probably enjoyed the break!) but it's been a bit of an emotional roller coaster the last few days!! Booked yesterday off to do some Christmas shopping otherwise known as self-mutilation! Walking back to the multi-storey car park with a load of shopping bags I was attacked by my ex-wife – fortunately there was a witness and it was captured on CCTV.

Followed quickly by:

Opps sorry pressed send prematurely. Well gist of it is in police station most of yesterday, hopefully they are going to arrest her and let me get on with my life! Meanwhile in the middle of it all my youngest daughter who lives with my ex-wife decided to make contact! Crazy day! Anyway as you can see I've got more baggage than Samsonite! Been to the Outlet shops today (a professional shopper I hasten to add) so now doing the wrapping!! Hope your weekend has been a bit calmer!☺

Demi was determined to respond fairly rapidly as she felt he needed support. She would need to quickly find the right positive fun balanced with some empathy.

Really sorry to hear that. I hope you are ok? I guess it was good to hear from your youngest daughter in amongst all the other muddle?! Have been stuck in all day doing 'real' housework after the mess from having my floor laid (still tempted to put a smutty comment)!☺ My sister-in-law is taking me out on the 'razz' tonight starting at Aruba!! Wish me luck?!! Think I may be nursing a slight hangover tomorrow!☹ Could do with hitting the shops myself as getting withdrawal symptoms as seems like ages since I've been.☹☹ I hope you enjoyed your Outlet shopping. Did you get your usual Diesel jeans? What have you got planned for tomorrow? Sounds like you need a Delilah to go with your Samsonite – sorry it's the best I could do!! D☺

Demi was filled with delight and a desire to be by Josh's side when she received his reply. She didn't have to wait long for it and it was upbeat and full of fun. When would she get to be with him? How much longer would it be before he invited her for coffee?

OMG this wrapping is a nightmare!! Carpet looks like pink crumpled blooming paper!! I've bought about 40 silly things to go in a stocking... Bad move!! So you're out on the razz then – you probably deserve it after all that cleaning!! How were your do's this week? I left the staff party at 10.30 how bad is that!! Nearly bought some Diesel's (good memory by the way) then was seduced by the sign saying that True Religion was coming shortly so held out!! Mind you I consoled myself with 2 shirts and a jumper from All Saints and unfortunately I don't mean the group!! Well while you're abusing your body tonight...I'm doing it next Friday, hopefully I'll pop down that gym!! Last 2 weeks of the old gym membership and then I need to find a new one from January, least I turn into a wobble bottom!!!☺

It had worked. She was pleased. Josh's text and spirits were lifted and his response was fun and lengthy and gave a positive vibe of wanting to 'chat'. There was some great content in it that required a considered response so Demi set about working on the right words, which took a while.

So New Year, New You, New Gym then is it?! After 3 portions of Xmas pud and custard this week & not a gym insight I bet my bottom will be wobblier than yours by January!! Black tie do was good except out of about 100 men there wasn't a decent one in sight – I could have stayed at home with cocoa & slippers after all!! Your staff party was that good then? Hopefully you can make up for it on Friday – where are you going? True Religion? Sounds like something Freddy Mercury would sing about! You do seem to do well at this shopping lark – I am really impressed!☺ Good luck with the wrapping!! (I've done all mine!!) Enjoy the gym!☺

You do make me smile...Here I am trying to feel sorry for myself and there you go spoiling it!!☺ If the truth be known I've kept myself away from anyone and everyone until court case in January least they get caught up in the ugliness of my ex-wife's world! Mind you bit concerned about shopping locally in case I get attacked again – hopefully the police will now be able to stop her! Anyway yes been going to the gym at all sorts of weird hours to avoid being attacked and obviously to hide the wobbly bits!! Anyway thanks once again for always putting a smile on my face...Ohh and wear your glasses there are nice men out there...Whether they are house and potty trained is another matter!!!☺

Not expecting Josh to reply, his text had come through while she was out for the evening. She was bowled over, filled with love, desire, concern and hope. She picked up on the message that he was in no place to start meeting up with anyone until he had sorted his life out. She was prepared to wait and would be there for him when he was ready. In the meantime she would continue being a friend and giving him support. Demi would not be able to respond until the morning.

She knew that Josh knew that she had been out and she also knew that he was in a better place now, so she need not worry about him. As much as she wanted to be there for him she wasn't and therefore she couldn't stop her life and let it completely revolve around a text relationship.

Demi had really enjoyed her evening out. Her sister-in-law Sarah was great company and they were both well overdue a few drinks, a chat and a good time. It took Demi a while to wake up Sunday morning. And when she finally surfaced she had a hangover for England! Pushing herself forward she was keen to focus on a reply to Josh before she got sucked in to her busy day.

Also Demi was excited. It was the weekend before Christmas, spirits were high and she was falling in love with Josh or the man behind the texts at least!! Brewing a large coffee and making two slices of toast (she needed the sustenance to ease her head and stomach); Demi set herself ready to work on her response.

Thanks for the advice re the glasses. I was obviously wearing the wrong ones the other night cos there was definitely some good "eye candy" last night albeit that most of them were still in nappies!!☺ Hey, you don't get to 40 something (sorry if I have just added you a few years!!), divorced with a couple of children without having some "stories" to tell. You should see the size of my library – so to speak!!☺ Thought I might wander into downtownsville later to get some fresh air (if you can call the drug laced air from there fresh!) and ease the slightly tight head!! Did you get your wrapping done? What have you got planned for today? Or should I say, where are you shopping today?

CHAPTER FOURTEEN
Hump Day

B EING TRUE TO her word Demi set off on the 10 minute walk to the local shops. The fresh air would be good as her head was a little sore. Having gathered a few bits and some last minute stocking filers Demi decided to treat herself to a nice coffee. It was when she sat down that she noticed that Josh had sent a reply.

Hey cheeky!! Mind the needles! I know you work for the NHS but it is rather taking your work home with you going to the local downtownsville! Have you had your inoculations? Got a phone call from the police last night at 3.30am. Once in a lifetime opportunity to pick my youngest daughter up in a silver blanket from Bournemouth!! Lots of drunken upset but clearly having a hard time, which is heart-breaking! Anyway just outside my adopted family's house waiting for my eldest daughter for our Xmas lunch. Hopefully I'll be wobbling out later!!☺

As she started to read it she couldn't help the big smile that spread across her face, the love emanated in her eyes, the desire through her body and the small laugh out loud. Then as she got to the middle part of the text her heart felt heavy. What must they all be going through? She wished she could just be there and put her arms around them.

Demi used her coffee time to compose her reply. She thought she would start by picking up on the attempt at humour that he had included at the end of his text.

I hope she (eldest daughter that is) doesn't take too long to cook and is worth the wait!!☺ Your youngest is clearly having a difficult time – at least she was able to rely on her Dad and you were there for her as hard as it must be for you too.

I've got a strong immune system so I'm sure I can survive "Downtownsville" for an hour.☺ Enjoy your Xmas lunch. And remember you'll need at least 2 lots of Xmas pud if you want to wobble more than me!!☺

Demi didn't get a response. No doubt Josh was taking full advantage of the time with his friends, who he was obviously close to and who gave him support.

As usual, as the new week crept along Demi couldn't get him out of her mind and by Wednesday she was desperate to know if he was ok. She thought she would send a short text with a happy message.

As she drove to work that morning she planned what she would write. As soon as she had grabbed a coffee from the dining room and reached her desk she sent Josh her text. Being Wednesday she thought she would use office terminology for the middle of the week as a basis.

Hey! Happy 'hump' day!! Hope you're having a good week & things have settled down a bit from the weekend. Enjoy the rest of the week. D☺

His reply, which didn't take long, was hilarious. Demi laughed and was equally embarrassed!

Hey you is that a rude expression.??? Meant something different I'm sure when I was younger you saucy devil!☺

She replied straight away feeling that an explanation was in order and still giggling. She couldn't wait to share this with the girls when they came in to work.

Sorry! As it's an 'office' expression I thought you would know it!! However the 'rude' version is much more fun!☺ That's going to make me giggle now for the rest of the day!!☺

Josh's reply made Demi pleased that she had sent her text this morning. She had made him laugh so job done.

So long as giggling is all you're getting up to on national 'hump' day!! No wonder that the NHS is in trouble... (Now I see why you've always got a shortage of beds...!) PS it did make me laugh thanks.☺

Demi could hear him, in his office, laughing over his coffee. She could see that big cheeky grin and she could feel the love waves vibrating, reaching out and joining them together.

Demi decided not to reply and to wait until Christmas Eve. She had remembered that Josh was going out on the Friday night so she would wait until Saturday morning to text. Two reasons, one it was Christmas Eve and two it meant she wouldn't have to wait all evening on Friday for a reply.

As she woke up on Saturday morning she wondered how he was feeling after his night out. Would he be ok, up early and out for a run or would he be feeling worse for wear and still in bed. She hoped the latter as it would hopefully mean he had 'let his hair down' and had a good time.

Hi! Happy Christmas Eve.☺ I hope you had a good time last night and that you are not suffering too badly today!!☺ I'm having a quiet day, bit of tidying & veg prepping for tomorrow then off to my sister's later for an open house party (I must remember to take the WII or I'll be in trouble – again!!) What are your plans? Let me guess?!! Some shopping, somewhere, at some time? D☺

The longer she waited for a reply the more she hoped he had a good time and was taking a while to come back to life. Either that or he had hit the shops early for those last minute presents. Eventually, the long awaited reply arrived.

Hiya...First hangover in 6 years!! I ran to get the car this morning then went back to bed... daughter is just dragging me to the pictures!! At least I'll be able to sleep!!! Boy I'm too old for this... it's for youngsters!! Have a great afternoon on the WII and a good day tomorrow!☺

Having kept herself busy Demi was out enjoying Christmas Eve with Aaron, Nadia and friends by the time his text arrived. It meant that she wasn't able to reply for a while. However, hearing from him warmed her through and helped her enjoy what she was doing even more. She could feel her shoulders relax and her smile grow.

Also, if he was at the 'pictures' he would have his phone off and wouldn't see her message until later and if he saw it before then he would not be able to reply until later. Having convinced herself that it would be ok to hold off replying for a while Demi then had an opportunity mid-afternoon to get a text sent. She had popped back home to pick up some bits before heading to her sister's for the evening and used this space away from everyone to send her reply.

Fabulous!! Let's hope you had fun when you remember it!!☺ Have a good sleep at the pictures (I think they call it the "movies" in the 21st century!!☺) My quiet day has ended up being a boozy lunch in the local beach pub with Aaron & Nadia and a couple of friends. Off to my sister's shortly for a boozy rest of the day/evening & tomorrow!!☺ Have a lovely time tomorrow and I hope Santa is kind to you. D☺

Demi was enjoying her Christmas this year. She was surrounded by her wonderful family and she had a love growing from a distance with a wonderful man whose attention she desired strongly. She realised she was beginning to know how this 'wonderful' worked, as at 5.30pm, cinema kicking out time, she received her reply.

Ok trendy it was called the flicks in my day!! How do you do it, all this booze and still go out to play?? Do you ever stop?? Anyway I've not been able to get much sleep as the movie was so action packed!! Good gig mind you! My daughter is talking of dragging me to a couple of our locals tonight, just what I need! I've just got 4 DVDs in for Christmas and would rather stay in and watch Planet of the Apes (I can relate to their cause!!!) Have a great night out and do everything I can't!!!☺☺☺

Demi had chance to read it, be pleasantly affected by his humour and the relaxed nature and feel of it. As she was busy with family fun she didn't have chance to spend time on a reply. She knew, from his text, that he was also busy and she wasn't worried about him. Therefore, she decided to save her reply for the morning and to use it to wish him Happy Christmas.

As usual, Demi was up early on Christmas Day. The excitement she always had when the boys were young and all the planning that went into the day hadn't left her yet. Chas was still asleep and she would wake him by 9am if he hadn't surfaced before then. Guests were due from about 11.30am onwards and there was church to get to by 10am. A first thing first though this year was sending a text to Josh. A reply would be like all of her Christmas's coming at once.

Ho ho ho! Merry Christmas! Hope you have a lovely day with lots of pressies.☺ Who won last night the DVDs or your daughter? I'm up and waiting for the day to start (I get a bit excited even though there's no-one else to be excited with as they're all still in bed!!) Have loads of fun!!☺☺

Father Christmas was definitely her best friend this year as, just a few minutes later, her phone 'pinged' with Josh's reply. She was already sure he would be up and about and finding things to keep him busy.

Hey saddo what you doing up so early after a heavy night!! Happy Xmas to you too! Know what you mean as waiting for my daughter to surface... Just going for a run because it's a bit boring on my own!! Well I won the boy vs girl DVD battle as we watched a true life film based on a chap who was Sadam Hussain's son's double!! It was riveting!! Anyway I hope this is not my last text... But if the turkey goes the wrong way today... Well we may be using the NHS services!!!☺

She was pleased he was still upbeat. This was his and his daughters' first Christmas under new circumstances. They all had obviously had a difficult year and it wasn't over yet. She also loved the humour in his message. She was excited and replied quickly.

The best way to hit a hangover is head on!! Might even go for 'hair of the dog'!!☺ Wow you sure have a great taste in DVDs! Let's hope Santa has spotted it!!☺ You could always lend it your satnav (the turkey that is so that it goes the right way)!! Enjoy your run.☺

Another quick reply from Josh followed, although a little less upbeat, she put it down to the fact he was rushing off out for a run. She also felt no need to respond and anyway she had to get cracking on with her busy day as she had 9 people turning up for dinner!

Cheeky!! Well hair of the dog I'm impressed!! I'm not doing any alcohol for another year I'm an old boy you know!! Well I'm booted and suited and just off around the mean local streets with my 80's music on my iPod... What life's come to ehh...Christmas day!!! Have a great day.☺☺☺

Christmas was always a special occasion in Demi's family. They all loved the excuse to spend quality time together and all enjoyed each other's company.

It also wasn't going to be long before Demi was off to South Africa for a month. And while this was incredibly exciting, as she would be spending time with her best friend Jenny, and having an adventure of a life time, she would also miss her family and worry about them. That made the time they had over Christmas very special.

Demi knew Josh was safe and well and would be doing his best to enjoy Christmas Day. She also knew that he wouldn't want or expect her to keep in regular contact with him. Feeling safe in that knowledge Demi decided that she could wait until Boxing Day before replying. That way she could check that his Christmas Day had gone ok and make sure he was still in a good place.

CHAPTER FIFTEEN
Bonkers and Brave

S O AFTER A VERY busy, boozy and lovely Christmas Day Demi's family decided to meet at the beach on Boxing Day. Demi had a well-deserved lie-in before dragging herself, in the freezing cold, to the beach. The sun was shining and it was a beautiful winter's morning, perfect for a lovely walk before reaching the café for a well-earned warm drink. It was while sitting in her car in the sunshine that Demi used the waiting time, having arrived early, to reply to Josh.

Hey! How was your day? Did your turkey go the right way? Got up a little worse for wear this morning so took a leaf out of your book and went back to bed!! Sat in my car next to the Beach at the moment waiting for rest of the family to arrive! Its blooming freezing – we must be bonkers!! D☺

She had to wait a while for his reply, which was ok as she was enjoying her walk and she didn't have chance to read it. She would have to wait until she got back home before having time to compose a response as she couldn't face the barrage of questions she would get from her nieces if she attempted to spend time on her phone replying to a text. They would tease her endlessly and she didn't want too many people to know about Josh yet. Demi did however manage to get a sneaky few minutes with Jaini to update her. It was lovely being able to share her enjoyment with someone.

Hey bonkers why freeze your bits off when you could be at the outlet shopping village with your daughter and millions of other idiots dying a slow suffocating death!!! Yesterday was fine, really proud of my daughter as she got us both through it followed by Planet of the Apes on DVD...Traditional Xmas I believe!!!☺

Demi enjoyed Josh's text even though she thought him barmy to have attempted shopping on Boxing Day - of all the days!

When Demi finally got home and replied she was amazed at the run of texts and banter that followed. Oh, how she so enjoyed those moments. How close it made her feel to him and how she wished she was with him in person, just to be able to reach out and touch him.................

Who's bonkers? Outlet shopping on Boxing Day - that's both bonkers & brave!! I hope it was worth the pain & you've picked up some good bargains!☺ Just got back home to face the mess from yesterday as it didn't get done before I went out & the boys still believe in fairies & are nowhere to be seen!!☺ Planet of the Apes? Really?? And on Xmas day!! D☺

Hey you...it gets worse...I'm at work!!!☺

You are incorrigible!!☺

Hey I'm a simple guy from Bombay... Not quite sure what that means....but class myself as a bit sad at the moment!!! Hoping for a good next year once my court case is out of the way next week!! Hope the cleaning up isn't too tiresome - have a good evening.☺ PS. Department store sales tomorrow... Fingers crossed that they have True Religion jeans reduced!!!☺☺☺

There was a simple guy from Bombay, who could go shopping for a whole day. And he made it his mission to earn lots of commission when he flogged it all on eBay!! Boom boom!!☺

Very good!! You should be on the two Ronnies!!☺☺☺

Sated, smiling and filled with the most wonderful pleasures Demi relaxed and enjoyed the rest of the Christmas bank holiday walking on a cloud; protected in a bubble filled with love and joy.

CHAPTER SIXTEEN
Mrs Motivator

ALTHOUGH IT WAS Friday and people were back at work with the Christmas bank holidays over, Demi really didn't expect to hear anything from Josh until Saturday, New Year's Eve, and she had intended waiting until then before texting him. Therefore it was a heart-warming surprise to receive a text mid-afternoon with Josh obviously still in a good place despite what he had looming the following week.

Hi has school broken up for you yet?? I've been out rocking... school boys night out Wednesday – started at the pub at 7.30pm and then an Indian...All done by 9.30pm!!! Hey we're a wild bunch aren't we!! Out again for a pizza with one of my ex-colleagues last night... Stayed out late until 10 o'clock!!! Hey do you think I'll make it through to Midnight for New Year's Eve with all this late night practice???☺

Demi's couple of days back at work had been busier than she had expected. Usually this time of year was good for catching up as it was normally a quiet time. However, this year, when she felt she needed the quiet catch up time more than ever, she hadn't been as lucky. Knowing that she was off for the month in February and wanting to make sure the decks were clear and tidy before she went, clearly added to the situation. Managers knew she was due to be off soon and because she was highly regarded they called on her more than ever now that the Director was back because they had no faith in the Director's way of working. This meant that anything and everything was going through Demi and she was the one having to manage everything upwards to protect the Department's reputation and maintain harmonised relationships.

Josh's texts gave her the light relief she needed and today was no exception. Smiling, warm and definitely in love she replied. He really knew how to rock!

Wow you really are rocking and setting the pace for us 'old birds' to follow!!☺ I've had a busy week and will be breaking up soon if I can force everyone out the door! I've instilled too much commitment in them!!☺ No doubt you'll be there dancing around (or in!) the fountain at midnight to Auld Lang Syne!!☺ Did you get your jeans the other day or are you off for more bargain hunting at the weekend?!! D☺

She was pleased that she had remembered about the jeans and that she had asked a question. Now, would he reply?

Demi heard her phone 'ping' and knew it was a message from Josh. She was busy finishing off at the office and decided to wait until she got home before reading it. She would use the drive back to imagine his reply and plan her retort.

Got my jeans thanks but now got buyers' guilt!!! Have a great new year.☺

Finally home and settling down for a comfy evening in Demi took opportunity to respond. She was sure they were going to have lots of banter over the New Year weekend and she was really looking forward to it.

Demi had made a plan with herself to keep things light, with no strings and just a little flirting until after the divorce proceedings. Then she would attempt to step things up a bit. Flirt a bit more and maybe if he didn't make the first move, she would. Although this wasn't her usual way, it was the way she had been so far in this relationship and sometimes, it paid to be brave and push your usual boundaries.

I have escaped the office at last! Thought about going to the gym – at least that exercised the mind!!☺ I'm sure the buyers' guilt won't last long when you're 'strutting your funky stuff' in front the ladies!! Have been invited out with my sister and family tomorrow night and I'm not sure that it's for me. They want to go to the local pub that I haven't been to for about 15years!!☺ The alternative is spending the night with Graham Norton & a glass of wine – how "rocking" is that??!! You have a great New Year too. D☺

.....and......nothing! Soon, too soon, it was bedtime and Demi had received no reply. She convinced herself that maybe he had gone out, which she hoped he had, or maybe he was watching a film with his daughter. Either of these could be likely and that was ok. Demi was sure she would get a reply in the morning telling her all about it and the mystery would be solved. In her darkest moments she feared the worse, what if his ex had done something nasty again? What if one of the girls was playing up? Oh, how she hated not knowing.

Demi had ended up staying in on New Year's Eve and had whiled away her time during the day at the gym and out shopping. Work had not been its usual satisfyingly challenging place the last couple of weeks and Demi didn't much like how things appeared to be developing. The retail therapy was a good distraction along with having her holiday to shop for and look forward to.

New Year's Day came and went with still nothing from Josh. Demi continued to busy herself, seeing family and doing all the usual domestic stuff. Only this weekend it all felt a bit of a blur and that she was on auto pilot. How can her mood change so much from the weekend before when she was walking on cloud nine. Now she felt like she was swimming through treacle.

By the morning of the Bank Holiday Monday Demi could wait no longer. She had to find out what was going on. If he wanted to end the relationship with the New Year then fine. She would get the 'message' if he didn't reply again. So taking the bull by the horns she went for it.

Hey quiet you how's your weekend going? I'm feeling smug right now as I've been to the gym twice already in this year!! So unless you can beat that then you have also won the wobbly bits competition as I have now wobbled my wobbly bits away!!☺ How was your New Year rave? Did your practicing pay off? I was tucked up in bed by 10.30 after having a naff week last week (full of self-pity & grumpiness!) so sat myself down, gave myself a strong talking to, pulled my socks up and put myself back on track!!☺☺ How are you doing? Hope you have a good day! D☺

Now she needed to busy herself, big time! Then, just as she was up to her eyes in cleaning the bathroom, always a good distractor, she heard that familiar sound. Rushing to remove the rubber gloves and grab her phone she started to get mixed feelings about what she read. Yes, it was upbeat and fun, only there was also a tinge of sadness beneath it all. Demi sat and read it a few times, wanting to feel his pain so that she could take it away from him.

Why were they both being so lonely when they could be together enjoying each other's company and sharing each other's darker and deeper moments, helping each other through the difficult times, together and in person, instead of via universal wave lengths?

Hey you or should I say Mrs Motivator!! Your texts do make me smile! I probably need some of your magical talking too after this week!! Well, being ultra-competitive I'm going to try & beat you on all counts!! Been running twice in New Year as new gym doesn't open until Thursday!! Went to join gym on Friday night and feeling sorry for myself walked past the pub and got sucked in....4 bottles of beer and an hour later (yes I made it right up to 8.30pm!!) and a friend's wife drove me to another friend's house who looked after me for the night!! As for New Year well.....I've rented everything going in Blockbusters so Barry Norman (is he still around??) watch out!!☺☺☺ Hey do I win the last chocolate brownie??☺

In a bid to keep both of their spirits up Demi put her best efforts into her response. And, thankfully, it appeared to work.

What no shopping??!! No wonder the Prime Minister was so subdued yesterday with his New Year speech!!☺ And what with helping yourself to that many bottles of beer!! You're lucky it was a friend's wife who found you otherwise you could have been looked after by Her Majesty!!☺ Happy to share my magic as long as I don't have to wear a lime green leotard! – It's not my colour!!☺ And of course you can have the last chocolate brownie.☺

Thank you......For always making me smile.☺☺☺

Oh boy! She desperately wanted to make him more than smile. If they could be this good for each other via text just think what they could do if they were physically together. Bringing herself back to reality, Demi decided to leave it there, on a high. She would save her next text for Wednesday morning, court day!

CHAPTER SEVENTEEN
Pistol in your Pocket

H *I. BEST OF luck today. Hope all goes well. D☺*

And this made it all worthwhile.

Thanks D your text means a lot to me.☺

All day Demi couldn't shake Josh from her mind. She kept picturing the various possible situations at the court. Was he in the dock? Was he being pressed under questioning? How was his ex reacting? Were his daughters there and witnessing it? Did Josh have anyone with him for support? When would she hear from him? Should she text first or wait for him to reach out to her when he was ready? How she hated feeling so far apart from him especially when she wanted to be closer than ever.

Somehow Demi knew to give him some space and she was pleased that she had as, finally, two days later she got some of her answers.

Hi u how's it going – well had a jolly rotten week! Court went in my favour if you can call a several £k settlement that. My ex-wife wants an income until I die though so I now go to appeal in February for another two days!! Still maybe then I can start a new fresh chapter. Started my new gym this week as there is a lot of work to do on this body after the xmas indulgence!! Hey guess I must be racking up those chocolate 'feel sorry for myself' brownies... How's your week been??☺

Demi hadn't been at work long and was heading for a meeting when Josh's text arrived. She only had chance to quickly read it and heave a sigh of relief at hearing from him and there having been no excessive dramas. She would have to wait before she could reply. At least she could plan her response while she was in the meeting.

She had herself been in court, tribunal court, for the last two days, so she had some degree of empathy. Demi felt that she wanted to challenge Josh a bit to help him find something to celebrate from the ordeal and get him moving out of his 'feel sorry for myself' message.

Luckily her meeting didn't take long and Demi used the early finish to grab a coffee and tap in her reply.

Good to hear you've had a reasonable outcome this week! At least you know the worst case scenario pending the outcome of the appeal. Sounds like you've got a choice – lots of chocolate brownies & lots of gym or less chocolate brownies & less gym – I know what I would do!!☺☺ I've had 2 days in tribunal court this week. It all went well & I'm positive about the outcome although we won't hear for a few weeks yet. It will be a good one to win though so keep your fingers crossed!! So what are you doing to celebrate your "in my favour" settlement? And don't say eating more chocolate brownies & watching more DVDs as that will not be acceptable!! D☺

Feeling sure she wouldn't hear further from Josh until later that evening Demi concentrated on her day. When her phone signalled a message 20 minutes later she didn't rush to it as she was sure it wouldn't be from Josh. When eventually she did get to it she was surprised to see it was from him.

Hi Ms Brownie!! No celebrations yet as I've been warned that the appeal will be worse...!!! I'll be out on the town next Friday when I've had time to lick my wounds and slim down in to my designer jeans!! I've got my fingers and toes crossed for you!☺

Unfortunately, due to the busyness of her day Demi was going to have to wait until she got home before she had time to reply. At least she would be home early as she was off to the Doctors for holiday jabs at 3pm. Boy, how she wasn't keen on injections – never mind, it was all for a good cause after all!

When Demi eventually got home, after needing more injections than she'd bargained for, she set about drafting a reply to Josh. She was getting good at finding the right balance between empathy and motivation, despite his ability to continually challenge her on this. Eventually she was happy with her result.

Ms Brownie!! Is that PC??!!☺ Sorry, I thought from your first text that you had appealed and now from your second text and re-reading I guess she has appealed!! Anyway, you still need to use getting through this week as an excuse to celebrate a little bit otherwise the bit that you have achieved will go unnoticed. If I was you I would treat myself to a larger pair of designer jeans!!☺ Have just got back from the Drs and feel like a pin cushion!! Went to get a yellow fever jab for my pending holiday and ended up having Tetanus, Diphtheria, Polio & Typhoid as well!!!! I'll need to block the holes up otherwise the wine might leak out!!☺

And how elated she was, and more in love, when only 10 minutes later she received his reply.

You make me laugh!!! See you're so greedy you want everything!!! So where are you going then????☺

Her reply needed to be quick as she was getting ready to go out and was being picked up in ½ hour. She got excited every time she spoke about her pending holiday. Add that to the excitement of texting Josh and Demi was jumping around all over the place.

Off to South Africa for 25 days on 3rd Feb & can't wait.☺ Staying with Jenny Finan who you may remember from Insurance 4 U. We are best buddies. We are going to Victoria Falls in Zambia/Zimbabwe for a few days & they won't let you in if you haven't had a yellow fever jab!!

Just as she was almost ready to rush out of the door Demi's phone 'pinged'. She knew it was Josh and hoped that she would get away with another quick response as she was running to the car. Luckily, as she guessed from his text, Josh was also out for the evening.

Wow you lucky 'Brownie'!! Just stepping into the High Sheriff's residence for an equally stimulating evening!!!!☺

I hope you've got your spurs and lasso with you and make sure you keep your pistol in your pocket!!☺ Have a good evening. D☺

Hoping that her comment wasn't too risqué and that he would enjoy receiving it as much as she had enjoyed sending it, Demi skipped out the door.

CHAPTER EIGHTEEN
Perception and Praise

RESISTING TEMPTATION to text to find out how his evening had gone Demi set about her weekend. Her mind constantly distracted by thoughts of Josh, what he was doing and who he was with, Demi attempted to do her weekend chores.

Having her holiday looming and things to focus on helped to get her through the hours of waiting to hear from Josh.

Then, just as she was giving up hope of hearing from him again this weekend, and she had settled down to Sunday TV and ironing, a message arrived. Demi read it and laughed out loud.

Hi how was your weekend? I was badly let down by you on Friday!! Having taken my cowboy outfit to see the High Sheriff (oh by the way I am a little worried at the ease you tend to jump for these particular types of outfits!!)... Well guess what it was, all swords and men in tights...!!! I was so embarrassed..!! And there I was thinking you were a woman of the world.☺

Keen to reply and keep the fun going Demi stopped ironing and focused on the right words to use. Making sure to end with a question in the hope that it would encourage a quick response and more fun conversation.

Clearly my world is very small☺ surely though my version was far more fun!! (Well it was for me!!☺) Men with spurs & pistols vs men with tights & swords – no contest!!☺ I have been packing all weekend as under orders to take extra luggage for Jenny. She has a flat here that she rents to my niece & has everything stored in the loft. I have raided the loft to find a list of things she wants me to take out with me!! Also I am suffering from the side effects of my cocktail of jabs & feeling fluy & sorry for myself. Hope you've had a good weekend ☺ what's your week ahead got in store? D☺

Her ploy worked as it wasn't long before he replied.

Sorry to hear you're feeling dickie! London tomorrow working for IBSA boring! Promised myself a night out on Friday night to keep me going...Probably only local with my daughter. Ease myself back into the real world slowly!! How about you?☺

She sensed a bit of sadness in his reply and she wondered what else she could do to encourage him to turn to her for some company. They could meet for a drink mid-week for example, which would at least break his week up and give him something to look forward to. It didn't have to be 'heavy' and could be as friends with no stings. Demi would settle for that – short term!

Feeling frisky, full of love and fun Demi replied. This time, against what she wanted to do, she ended giving him licence not to reply until the end of the week. If he did reply it would be a bonus; she was beginning to understand the rhythm of their relationship.

Oh, Dickie doesn't mind. Its Fred & Joe we have to worry about!!☺☺ Thankfully I'm local all week. It'll be a busy one though catching up on missed days last week & sorting out the havoc the Director is creating!! Enjoy your week – it'll be Friday before you know it!! D☺

It was Aaron's birthday that week so Demi used this as a good distraction from Josh. She used a couple of late night shopping opportunities to pick up some small gifts and to shop for party food. She had arranged a small family gathering on Thursday to celebrate the event. They all had a lovely time and the distraction worked very well.

Demi had been right about Josh not texting again until the weekend, although he kept her waiting until he had been out for the night before texting. She was pleased with this though as she felt it meant that she was in his thoughts. It was obviously difficult for him to text at times and he was using any chance that he had. After all she understood how difficult it was to find time to plan a reply and to keep things a secret. This wasn't a relationship to be shared with too many others, it was our secret. Of that Demi was sure.

Hi u how's your week gone? Mine has been crazy on both a work and personal front!! Anyway really rocked tonight... Drink in the local pub with some friends from work then Dad's cabs duties!! Just eating a really naughty muffin in McDonald's waiting for my drunken daughter to decide whether she wants a lift home!! I'm thinking of charging, what do you reckon my services are worth????!!

Demi's week had been pretty bad. Nothing much usually got her down and she couldn't really put her finger on it. All she knew was that her boss returning from maternity leave was not having a positive impact on the team or the organisation. Demi also felt that her boss was jealous of the reputation Demi had and Demi could sense some spiteful behaviour taking place that was meant to find ways of damaging Demi's career. Little did Demi know at this point how this was going to play out over the coming weeks.

Hi. My week has been pretty rubbish & I'm glad it's the weekend!! Your services are only worth what someone is willing to pay & I guess when it comes to a group of youngsters on a night out it'll be a while before you get your 1st million!!☺ Gym, shopping & housework planned for the weekend. What are you up to? D☺

This time it was Demi's turn to feel sorry for herself only she wanted to hide this from Josh if she could. Clearly he was more perceptive then she'd given him credit for.

Hey u what went wrong this week ☹ it's not like you to let things get you down!! Just been seeing how the other half live... been to Tesco's and bought a car air freshener to find somewhere warm to hang out whilst these juniors are out rocking!! Boy its cold out tonight!!☺

Having used the 'waiting for a reply' time to get ready for bed. Demi was snuggled in the warm when Josh's text arrived. She decided she would weave this into her reply to see what, if any, effect it would have.

Trust you to choose the coldest night of the year to be loitering around street corners!! Make sure you keep your anorak done up or you might be accused of all sorts!!☺ I'm ok; it's just a little blip & nothing that a glass of wine (or 2) can't sort out!!☺ Thanks for asking. I won't tell you that I am snuggled up in bed under a lovely warm duvet as that wouldn't be fair.☺ Hope you get home soon.

Clearly not the effect she had hoped for! He obviously took the wrong hint deciding to leave her alone to go to sleep! With the lack of response by Saturday lunchtime Demi decided she would have to find out how his night had ended as she couldn't face going a whole weekend without hearing from him again. And she was pleased with her gym achievements and wanted to share this with someone, him.

Morning!! I hope you've managed to thaw out and get a few hours' sleep!! I have done the gym thing for today & even managed a 10 min run (1ˢᵗ run I've done in 9 months).☺ I'll soon be out pounding the streets again - deep joy!!☺ I've sorted my washing, done a quick tidy up and now heading into town for some retail therapy - very exciting!!☺ What are you up to? Hope you have a good day. D☺

Even from a distance and using the universe's wave lengths she could attract the results she wanted. If only it worked every time!

Hey well done you on the exercise....I'm leaving it until tonight!! Honest!! Anyway if you can't beat them join them... Ended up going into a Thai restaurant with my daughter and friends in the end ...Dreadful place full of young people!!☺

Anyway round my Mum's back on project divorce. Only 3 weeks to go!! After spending several £k on legal fees thus far have to find another few £k for next month so this week has been a bit interesting and stressful!! Anyway off on my ward rounds (thought I'd try an NHS link!!) tour around my long list of friends this afternoon! You're sounding more chippa today which is nice to see.☺

Demi felt the warmth from Josh's praise on the exercise and chatty cheerful reply. He had displayed good empathy in the way he had picked up on her down moments and taken his turn in offering support and showing that he cared.

Determined to keep busy and not show how keen she was by replying too quickly, Demi decided to wait until she had completed her shopping trip before she composed her response. Also, she knew he would be concentrating on his divorce papers and she didn't want to intrude and distract him. She only hoped he would manage to keep his spirits up.

2 pairs of shoes; 2 dresses; 2 sets of jewellery; 1 handbag + loads more "holiday essentials" and I thought I should head back home!!☺ A glass of wine tonight and that should complete the cure!!☺☺ I'm sorry that you're still having a tough time. 3 weeks will be over in no time and you'll soon be free to move on to the next chapter of the life & times of Mr B.☺ Hope you enjoyed your home visits and I'll be checking up to make sure you get to the gym later. Have fun. D☺

What Demi hadn't expected was complete 'radio silence'. Especially when she thought they were taking their 'friendship' to a stronger, closer place. She was desperate to know how he was and to know that he wasn't alone with his sadness. She was pleased she had added that she would be checking up on him as this gave her an excuse to text again.

Demi had started her Sunday at the gym and had met up with friends for lunch and a walk along the beach. This had kept her busy and used up a few hours. By early evening she could wait no longer. She couldn't risk having to wait until next Friday to see if he managed to spare her a thought. Yes, she knew he was having a hard time. Surely he realised that she was the one person where he could get some light relief and have a bit of fun.

So...I'm guessing you didn't make the gym last night & at best you went for a run this morning?? Right or wrong / hot or cold??☺ I managed a 15 min run this morning as well as all my other bits.☺ I've now decided I want to lose a couple of pounds before I go on hols especially as I have been asked to do a fashion show 10 days after getting back!! No pressure!! How's your day been? I've been a busy bee & have a few more things to do (like the ironing!!!) before bedtime! D☺

Getting stuck into the ironing and catching up on some recordings on the TV, Demi kept herself occupied. Considering recent timescales it wasn't too long before the reply came.

Hey ye of little faith...of course I made the gym last night... Then had an Indian at my adopted family's house to put the calories back on!! Slept for 12 hours last night which is unheard of!!! Having a mammoth DVD afternoon and evening with my daughter... Still get a bit embarrassed watching the rude bits with her (and I don't mean the kissing bits!!!) – reckon I should buy blockbuster shares given the number of films I rent!!☺

She could sense he was struggling to put on a brave face. The fact that he was staying close to home, watching movies was a sure sign he was in a low mood.

She could empathise with the 'rude bits' he referred to and decided to share this with him. Hopefully it would bring a smile to his face. She wasn't hopeful for a reply as she felt he was in one of his 'lonely' moods. Pressing send she knew, sadly, that it would be a long week untill Friday!

Hey, how did the Indian do that? Was he trained?☺ 12hrs sleep – wow, that's a bit greedy!!☺ There can't be many movies left that u haven't seen!! I know what you mean about the rude bits! Luckily for me Chas has his own TV in his room. The thing is I'm never too sure if it's the movie or him & his girlfriend I can hear through the wall!! And at what point to ask them to keep it down – so to speak!!☺☺ Enjoy your evening. D☺

CHAPTER NINETEEN
Little Chef Man

A ND INDEED IT was a very long week. The environment at work was becoming very challenging. Demi's team were very unsettled with the abrupt, abusive and unnecessary demands from the Director, who had no idea what she was doing. She kept changing her mind and calling time-wasting meetings that resulted in no outcomes. Senior Managers across the organisation were pulling their hair out in frustration. All of it impacting on Demi as the team and Senior Managers, all of whom trusted and respected her, were turning to her for support, guidance and someone to take their frustrations out on.

Demi had two days out of the office that week. One day to attend a regional Director's meeting and one day at a conference in London. Demi's Director did not attend the Director's meetings as she refused to drive, leaving the responsibility with Demi. Demi enjoyed the meetings and conferences and she was always keen to take an opportunity to get out of the office and do some networking. The only downside was what Demi had to come back to with the ciaos the Director created when Demi was away.

Demi's influencing, calming and mediation skills were being used to full capacity, which was extremely exhausting. On top of all that Demi still had her everyday work to do and her month off was only two weeks away. There was a lot to get through!

Demi's second day out that week was at a conference in London. She had gone with her favourite colleague, Dyna. Dyna was one of Demi's peers and she understood the pressure that Demi was under. Dyna, being a special colleague, was one person who Demi had fully shared her relationship with Josh.

Demi was excited about their London trip. They were going to Tower 42 and had planned to get there earlier than needed so that they could visit the

Champagne Bar. What a fantastic view, sipping champagne, looking out across London and the Thames. Just what the Doctor ordered. Dyna was great fun and they had a fabulous time.

Eventually it was Friday and Demi wondered how long she would have to wait for Josh's text or whether she would give in and text first.

Demi was very pleasantly surprised when mid-afternoon her phone signalled the arrival of a text. She was in a meeting and couldn't look at it straight away. She just knew it was from Josh and was immediately filled with a soft smiley glow and began to sit back, relax and drift off into a world of Josh.

Forty Five minutes later, running back to her office, grapping a nice coffee on the way, Demi excitedly sat down to open and read the text.

Hi u how's your week been? A bit better than last week I hope? I've been all over the country so am going to call myself 'international man of mystery'! Off to Stratford upon Avon for the weekend (after answering 7 solicitors' letters round my Mum's!)...I'd love to pretend I'm going for the Shakespeare culture...In truth I'm visiting an old mate from school! What have you got planned??☺

Demi was pleased that he seemed in a better mood and disappointed that he was away for the weekend in case it meant he wouldn't text. Although she was pleased he was doing something with a friend instead of being alone. As long as it wasn't a female friend!

His divorce was obviously complicated and serious as it was taking a lot of effort for Josh to get through it all. She wished it was all over for him and worried about how bitter it was likely to end up making him. Demi hoped that, in time, he would be able to put it behind him and move on. It took a while before she could reply as within minutes of getting to her office Demi had a queue of people waiting to see her and then it was time to pick her son up and drive home.

Demi was excited to be able to tell Josh about her trip to London and to keep him guessing about a conversation she'd had with Dyna. As soon as she got through her front door Demi replied.

Hey, International Man of Mystery, you sound set for a fun weekend after a busy week.☺ My week's been much better thanks. Taunton Wednesday & then Tower 42 London yesterday, which was fab!☺ Had a glass of bubbly in the champagne bar on the 42nd floor & then dinner in the Gary Rhodes restaurant on the 24th floor.☺☺ Just a shame it was a work outing!! My colleague insisted on telling me 2 things that I needed to do – 1 was a PhD & the other cannot be repeated!!☺ I'm sure I'll achieve the PhD in the next 5 yrs. I'm not so sure about the other!! Honestly, solicitors!! They certainly know how to make an industry out of anything!! Most men who travel a lot have a 'women in every port'. You seem to have an 'old mate from school'!! Or is that part of the 'mystery'?? Have a great weekend. D☺

She was giggling as she pressed send as she just knew this would make him smile. She loved an opportunity to be a bit 'flirty' and she hoped he would pick up on it. And it seemed to work.

Hey cheeky!!! So in addition to being a model, cowgirl you're now a brain box as well!!! Quite a catch!! I'll ponder on my journey up country as to your second challenge!!! Should make the journey go faster!!!☺ PS I'm more of a little chef man myself!!!☺☺

Demi was busy getting ready to go out. After the week she'd had a glass of wine and fun with friends was much needed! It was therefore a while before she had chance to drop him a quick text in response. She loved his reference to Little Chef and she couldn't resist playing on that in her reply.

Is that u admitting to wearing pinnies & funny hats or being short & fat??☺☺

Knowing that he was far from being short and fat Demi knew that her reference would not offend him. Aware that he had a busy weekend planned Demi was prepared to wait until Sunday for a reply. She told herself that she would give him until about 6pm on Sunday before she would give in, again.

Demi set about keeping herself busy for the weekend. She spent the time shopping and packing for her holiday. When Jenny had left the UK she had left behind a number of her belongings that were secured in the loft of the flat that Jenny now rented out. Demi looked after this for Jenny. Jenny had asked Demi if she could go through the loft to find some clothes and personal items that Jenny wanted and take them out to South Africa with her. This meant Demi needed to go around to Jenny's flat to access the loft and search for the things her friend wanted. These then needed to be packed into suitcases ready to take. Along with this Demi also needed to book extra luggage space with the airline she was travelling with. All this was beginning to make Demi panic as she was running out of time and worrying about how she was going to get it all to London.

Demi's Friday night had been fun. Luckily she hadn't got home too late as her sleep was disturbed in the early hours when her son and friends rolled in, drunk.

Saturday morning Demi woke feeling very tired, worried about work and now worrying about her travels Demi was beginning to feel under pressure and she had a lot to do this weekend. It was only the thought of sitting by the pool with her best friend, sipping cocktails, that was keeping her going. As she settled in front of Sunday night TV with a much deserved glass of wine Demi was excited to hear her phone 'ping' with a message. Suspecting it was her son wanting a lift somewhere she was delighted to see it was from Josh and it was almost an essay of school boy excited tales. Demi couldn't help being transported from her worried mood as she read it.

Hi u how's your weekend so far?? I'm refreshed, full of real food, not the usual micro wave meals!! Spent yesterday afternoon & evening sleeping (needed it big time!!) & then had a mega breakfast, then lunch.... And tonight another mega meal!!! Ohh what it is to have friends who look after you & feel they have to help u put on weight because you're looking skinny!!! Going to audition as a telly tubby!! Confession time, only got one run in this weekend so going to feel guilty & hold back on the 'chocolate in front of telly' syndrome tonight!! Go on put me to shame!! Got 2 interviews this week which is a bit hectic trying to remember which is which... Ones for the circus & the other for the financial services industry. Not sure about either of them – just seemed like a good idea at the time!

She immediately set about drafting a reply. Wanting to enjoy the things he had told her and wanting to let him know how she was feeling as well, being careful not to dampen his mood.

Hey, u sound chilled & full of energy.☺ That's what friends are for!! I'm intrigued with the interviews – circus?? I wish you the best of luck & look forward to hearing the outcome. Which telly tubby are you going for? I can only remember tinky winky & I'm not sure that's the most flattering!!☺ I'll let you off the gym as I only made it once this weekend & nearly didn't do that after 4 drunken lads crawled in at 3.30am!!! Beginning to get very nervous about my travels. How am I supposed to get 3 suitcases to Heathrow on my own? And I'm not sure the coach will let me on with them all yet!! Oh well, I'm a big girl now so a couple of deep breaths & a flutter of eyelashes should do it.☺ Sunshine & cocktails to look forward to. Go easy on the chocolates!!☺

Demi waited for the reply, certain that it would come, if not tonight because he was out then definitely tomorrow morning. By Monday lunchtime she was very disappointed not to have heard from him. She began to wonder if he was relieved she was going away for so long as it would give him chance to stop the intense texting.

Demi really was in a strange place, with so many different emotions running through her. Excited about her holiday, yet nervous about her journey. Concerned about work, yet loving her job. In love with Josh yet no confidence in his feelings and the strength of their relationship.

CHAPTER TWENTY
Disturbed Nights

FINALLY IT WAS Friday and Josh's dutiful Friday text arrived. Demi was pleased she had restrained herself from texting first.

Hi how's your week been? So when is this holiday that requires all the bags for?? Had a mad week 2 interviews hundreds of miles and no lunch for the last few days.... Man cannot live on bread alone so I've survived on Costa's specialty – triple choc chip muffins!!! Can thoroughly recommend it!!☺

Exasperated by yet another difficult week Demi wanted to share. Keeping it light hearted she also managed to get in a question (her tried and tested way of prompting a response) and a bit about her holiday. She wasn't sure that he had picked up on her holiday properly as he was, quite rightly just now, focused on his own issues.

Hi – my week?! Will you promise to visit when I'm sent down for murder??!! This time next Friday I'll be on the plane ready for take-off!! 7 more sleeps!☺☺ How did the interviews go? When will you hear the outcomes? Which one will you choose when you get offered both?☺ It's the blueberry ones that do it for me!! D☺

What are the visiting times – is it a full search or a gentle frisk?? It is important when visiting a prison I understand!! Don't want either job but must get out before I kill someone!!☺ You jammy devil one week to go ehh!! How long are you away for??☺

She was surprised by his flirty reply and it made her giggle. Her question had worked and his response to it was interesting as Demi had assumed his job move was about furthering his career and not because he was unsettled. And he asked about her holiday, at last it was sinking in.

Demi hoped that they were getting into an evening of quick fire, chatty texts. She set about doing a quick reply on that basis and couldn't resist continuing the innuendos.

Sounds like we could be going down together!!☺ I get back in the UK on 28th Feb so away for 25 days – mind you I deserve it – even if I do say so myself!!☺

She was therefore disappointed not to get a reply. By Saturday morning she was beginning to go through all of those agonising thoughts, again. Was there a problem with one of his daughters? Had his ex done something horrible? Was he ok?

Demi was relieved to get a text later in the afternoon and upset that her fears for Josh had been realised.

Boy had a night of it last night – youngest daughter who is still living with my ex rang at 1am as she had left home & was distraught – so I was sat in the freezing car (again!) for much of the night sorting the pair of them out!! Any room in one of those 3 suitcases that I might come with you?? PS Why do you need 3 suitcases?? No running water where you're going!!☺

It was Demi's Mum's birthday and the family were gathered for an afternoon tea party. Being Daughters it had fallen to Demi and Jaini to organise the event, prepare the food and do all the serving and cleaning up. They enjoyed doing this together and despite it being a family mayhem they all had a wonderful time.

Demi was out when Josh's text arrived. She had read it and had to wait until she got home before she could reply as she felt it needed concentration and was not something that she could do on the hoof. She would also need to wait until her great nephew was asleep as Demi had offered to babysit so that her niece could go out for the evening.

She was relieved that at least no-one had been hurt and his words had made Demi fall even more in love with him. He was clearly a kind, caring, family man, who took the responsibility for his children very seriously. He had even managed to speak to his ex after everything that he had been through. Demi knew how tough that must have been.

She was touched that he wanted to jump into one of her suitcases and laughed at his sudden realisation that she was taking 3 suitcases!

Demi took advantage of time when her great nephew had fallen asleep after his tea. She was not sure how long the sleep would last and what sort of night she was in for. Usually when he was at home he was a good sleeper and she wondered if being in a strange place would interrupt his usual good pattern.

Oh dear! Doesn't sound much fun! I'm sure I can find room for you in 1 of them. 2 of the suitcases are for Jenny, my friend who I'm visiting. She has put in an order for me to take her some things!! Had a busy afternoon organising a birthday party for my Mum and now I've been left holding the baby tonight as have my 10mth great nephew staying!! I will be the one disturbed in the early hours tonight. Does it ever stop?.?!!☺ Hope you have a better night tonight. D☺

Josh had obviously been busy working, again, as his reply was sometime later.

Hi u is it all quiet on the western front so far?.? My, you're brave looking after a 10 month old baby!! My teenage daughters are enough of a handful!! Just sat in watching trash TV and practicing my speech that I'm giving to 133 16 year olds on Tuesday!!

Demi replied, feeling quite tired by this point. And on reflection, after pressing send, she realised she had forgotten all her own rules about asking a question and setting up a reason for him to reply.

Hey. You do do some crazy things!☺ They say you should never work with animals or children – they are one of the same in my book!! Baby is asleep bless him & I'm just settling down to a bit of Jonathan Ross before bed.☺ Hope your night remains quiet. D☺

Demi was not surprised that she didn't get a reply or hear anything at all the next day. She realised that he had more important things that he needed to do. Demi remembered he had mentioned that he was doing a presentation on Tuesday so she already had in mind to text him 'Good Luck' wishes if she didn't hear from him beforehand. This would give her an excuse for texting that she could justify well.

CHAPTER TWENTY ONE
Holi-Holiday

DEMI HAD DEVELOPED sore eyes while at work on Monday and had been advised to go to the eye hospital. They had diagnosed ulcers brought on by the use of contact lenses. She had been trying out contact lenses so that she could use them on holiday. After much toing and froing between the Pharmacy, Opticians and eye hospital, Demi was told no more contact lenses for at least a month. She had planned to treat herself to some posh designer sunglasses while she was wandering around the airport. Her holiday was definitely becoming a much needed remedy for a number of things.

Tuesday morning arrived and on getting in to work Demi sent a good luck text to Josh. Feeling well and truly sorry for herself she was convinced, before sending it, that Josh would not reply.

Hi. Hope your week has started well. Good luck with your speech today! My week is different as went to the eye hospital yesterday & have a virus in both eyes & 2 ulcers in my left eye!!☹ Sunshine & cocktails cannot come quickly enough!☺ Have a good rest of the week. D☺

Straight away – woohoo!

Hey poor you - just here practicing my speech – scary scary!!! Hope your eyes are ok - must have been since you saw me!!!☺

Demi was surprised that Josh was nervous as she thought that he would enjoy doing speeches and presentations. Maybe he would enjoy it when he got started.

With very sore eyes and lots to do Demi immersed herself in her work and colleagues. Her team were very fearful of her taking time off as they knew that they would get no support from the Director. They were also worried about the damage the Director would do while Demi was away.

Demi was finishing work on Thursday as she was flying on Friday. Having been too busy to really think about texts to or from Josh, Demi had pushed to the back of her mind that she would text him from the airport, as it was her turn to reply. Therefore she was really delighted to receive a text from Josh on Thursday afternoon and couldn't wait to finish work and get home so that she could concentrate on reading it and replying.

Hi u not long to go now. Bet you're excited!! How are your ailments? Are you ok to fly?? Obviously this is genuine concern as opposed to a selfish desire to take your place!!!☺ Thought I'd get in early today with a bon voyage message in case you and your 300 suitcases were up early at silly o'clock tomorrow!!! Have a great time, when you get back I'll be about a £1m poorer....And that would be a good result!!!☺

Hi. Finished work at last!! Ailments all on the mend thanks and fit to fly – sorry!! Thanks for your bon voyage message. Me and my many suitcases leave around 12pm ready for check in at 3pm and flight at 6pm. So if you want to squash in a suitcase you've got until 3pm!!☺ Should arrive in Jo'burg around 6.45am on Saturday – what a way to end the week!!☺ How was your speech? Keep focused on the "new you" that is soon to emerge.☺

Demi was really touched that he was wishing her 'bon voyage'. She got the feeling that he was going to miss her. He still had such a difficult time to go though and she would be sure to text him on the day of his court case. Not that she knew exactly when this was yet and would need to find out.

Demi was even more touched, and of course completely in love, when Josh text again early the next morning. Oh, how lovely it would be if they were going together. Was it too late to arrange something? Would he suddenly turn up in

South Africa and surprise her? Oh, how romantic. It could happen, couldn't it? After all it did in the movies.

Hi just wanted to wish you (yet again!!) a safe trip!! Remember tell the pilot to put a little more air in his tyres, especially with all those suitcases you're carrying. No taxi's into the townships after dark...No ...no...!! Have a good time.☺

Demi quickly replied in the hope she was catching him at a good time for a chat.

Thank you. I'm sitting on the suitcases struggling to close them at the moment!!☺ & they're bound to be overweight!! Have a good day. Hope you've got something exciting planned for the weekend. I'm still only a text away so no excuse for not keeping in touch!! D☺

Why am I not surprised about the suitcase!!☺ I'm thinking of going to see War Horse with my eldest daughter at the weekend...Couple of constraints mind you... Is a man allowed to cry???? Can one watch it in sunglasses so no one can see that you've got 'red eye'??? Is now the time to start singing I'm leaving on a jet plane...don't know when I'll be back again?? Or we're all going on a summer holiday??☺

Demi had jumped into the shower and was busy getting herself ready for her journey and had missed Josh's text coming through. She had checked her phone a couple of times and nothing was there. It wasn't until she sat down with a coffee that she noticed it. Disappointed that she had been delayed in responding, as by now Josh was probably busy at work, Demi replied.

She enjoyed his reference to song lyrics and loved an opportunity to have some fun with him.

War Horse should be fab.☺ Make sure you take a hankie (or 2!!) and you can always blame it on an eye virus!!☺ Not sure I'm quite old enough to remember the words to those 2!!! I'm more of a 'Hooray..Hooray... It's a holi-holiday' type of girl!!!☺

Demi set about the last minute preparations for her holiday in a mix of excitement and fear. This would be the second time she would be flying to South Africa on her own and she was prepared for being alone for the next 24 hours. She was worried about the number of suitcases she had, three big ones and her hand luggage! She wasn't sure what the coach driver would say and she couldn't wait to get to Heathrow to off load in the baggage drop off area. Then she would just need to keep her fingers crossed that they all arrived safely at the other end!

With all this worry about her travels Demi didn't have much chance to think about whether Josh would send her another text. Anyway, she knew he was busy at work and she would probably be on the plane before he finished for the day, with her flight being at 6pm.

CHAPTER TWENTY TWO
Sunshine and Cocktails

EVENTUALLY DEMI arrived in South Africa very excited at the prospect of being a few minutes away from seeing her best friend and glorious sunshine. Within two hours of landing Demi was hugged and kissed by her South African family, unpacked and sitting by the pool with a long cool cocktail. Wanting to share, and to let Josh know she had arrived safely, Demi sent him a text, her first from South Africa.

Hi u. Have arrived safely & sitting by the pool in bikini at John's (Jenny's brother's place) in Jo'burg. It is 25c already & rising!!☺ Have a good weekend & hope you enjoyed the movie.☺ D☺

Demi had already updated Jenny on this week's chapter of texts to keep her up to speed. Jenny knew Josh from their time when they had all worked at Insurance 4 U. Demi was pleased not to have to wait too long for a reply and immediately shared her excitement with Jenny. It was lovely to be able to do this together at the time it happened instead of by Skype once a week!

Hey u – weepy here.... That War Horse ehh!☺ Well look at you its -7c here and I've dug out my ski wear!!☹ Out man shopping for my daughter's birthday... god I hate it!! Have a dip for me. ☺

Demi had already decided that she wasn't going to spend the next three weeks constantly texting Josh. She knew that he had his appeal court case that coming week and she was determined to remember to text him on Monday with good luck wishes and then she would leave it and see what she got from him.

Demi easily relaxed and settled in to her holiday. Jenny had planned some exciting adventures, starting with a couple of quiet days by the pool and shopping. On Monday they were off to a lion park for the day and then on Tuesday the real excitement would begin with their trip to Victoria Falls. First things first though, at the start of the week, was a quick text to Josh.

Hi. Good luck with your court case this week. I hope it goes as well as can be expected. Take care. D☺

Thank you.☺

Then after not hearing anything from him the rest of the week or on Friday evening Demi needed to check he was ok. Especially considering what he had been through that week.

Demi herself had experienced a very different week. Starting off slowly adjusting to South African holiday life she and Jenny had flown to Zimbabwe for four days for an experience of a life time. And what an experience!

For some bazaar reason Demi and Jenny had chosen to go white water rafting down the Zambezi River. It turned out to be the most horrifying and scary experience ever. Made worse by the fact that Demi had a fear of water and couldn't swim!

Back at their hotel, still traumatised from their experience and sitting with a well-earned cocktail, Demi wanted to share with Josh. She was disappointed that he hadn't text on Friday night, although technically it had been her turn.

Howzit (SA for how are you)!! Its lekker (SA for fab) here. How was your week? I hope you're managing to find something to feel good about? We've just got back from white water rafting down the Zambezi!! If you're looking for a good DVD to watch I have it!! Our boat got flipped & it was all a bit dramatic. Bear in mind I don't swim & don't like water & if it wasn't bad enough that my makeup had already run & my hair had gone frizzy!! Not a good look. What are you up to? D☺

Demi wasn't surprised by the sad reply and did her best to be upbeat with him.

Hiya sorry had a bad week – got hit for a massive settlement and a monthly income for the ex! So I've done a bit of white water rafting myself this week!! Glad you're making the most of your time down there & we've had snow & it's still freezing!!☹

Oh dear I'm sorry to hear that. I'm taking comfort in a cocktail watching Ellies at the waterhole.☺ Maybe a beer by a warm fire & a polar bear might work for you?!!☺

CHAPTER TWENTY THREE
Double Whammy Wednesday

DEMI FELT SURE that she wouldn't hear from Josh until at least the next Friday. One, because she knew that he was in a hound dog mood and probably wouldn't be up to much and two, because Friday nights had become their routine. She was a bit nervous however about whether he would text on Friday as she wasn't sure how he would bounce back and if he would bother her while she was on holiday. She wondered how long she would leave it before texting him.

Demi was especially warmed and excited when she did receive a Friday message from Josh and she hoped that he was in a better place now from his ordeals of the previous week.

Hey u how's the safari gone this week?? Out for dinner with my daughter tonight as it's her birthday!!! I've landed myself in hot water as I threw out (inadvertently) her River Island gift vouchers with the wrapping paper!! Still, not quite as expensive as last Friday.☺ Hope you're having a good time – must only be another week to go??☺

So with the court case only being on the Friday last week explained why she hadn't heard from him until prompted by her on the Saturday. It also explained why he was still so raw in his reply. Demi hadn't realised that his court case hadn't been until the Friday. She had assumed it would be mid-week, like it was before.

Reading this new text Demi was pleased that Josh had something special to focus on even if he had thrown out the vouchers. It was a while before Demi could reply as she was out to dinner herself. When she got home she settled down to share with him some of the exciting things she had been doing and her plans for the next week. Although it was 10pm in South Africa, with the two hour time difference, it was only 8pm in the UK. Demi needed to reflect this in her text as Josh' evening would only just be starting.

Hi. Hope you have a great time tonight & make sure you spoil her. I'm sure she'll make you suffer for your (inadvertent) mistake!!☺ Have been to a game reserve/resort & Sun City this week. Jenny & I have been chasing around the safari in her Dad's Land Rover which has been great fun. Temperatures have been way in the 30s too!!☺ Have a friends/family party this weekend then off to Durban for a few days on Monday. Back in the UK on the 28ʰ. Have fun & enjoy the birthday celebrations. D☺

Demi was surprised to get a reply from Josh the next morning as she hadn't really expected or thought about when she might hear from him. She was enjoying how chatty they were and how excited she was every time they made contact. She felt so close to him and continued to dream about the time when they would physically be together. She was sure that he would make a move when she got back to the UK. The court case was over, the divorce settled, the girls in a better place and Josh moving forward. Surely he wouldn't make her wait too much longer. He had got her hook, line and sinker and she was already in love with and enjoying the prospect of what was to come.

Hey I'm exhausted reading your text!! Birthday meal went well & youngest daughter also slowly coming back into the fold so progress! Bombed a big interview this week even flopped the example questions that's how shattered I was after the court case!! Booked myself a getaway from it all cottage next month to chill & get some sleep. Enjoy the 4 x 4ing!!!☺

The only thing that worried Demi was the mention of him going away in March. Would this mean that she would have to wait for him to get back from it before they would meet? Could she wait much longer? Yes she could if it meant he would be in a better place emotionally. It would be important that he was able to accept what had happened and be ready to move on or their relationship would be doomed from the start. Demi could wait. She understood, and patience was a virtue. All good things came to those who waited after all.

And Josh would have to wait for a reply as Demi was busy travelling and partying and it would be a while before she would get some time to concentrate on it.

Hey. I'm pleased you had a good time & that relationships with your youngest are improving.☺ Time & patience are good healers. Sorry to hear about the interview, guess it's only to be expected with so much going on. Your escape to the cottage in March sounds perfect for recharging your batteries.☺☺ When & how long are you going for? D☺

She couldn't help laugh at his response. Demi was pleased that he appeared to be happy and in a good mood. And she was most definitely in love.

Hiya well never a dull moment in my life!! Met my youngest for lunch for the 1st time in 7 months yesterday......Talking so much I walked out without paying....Lady chased me out of the pub – how embarrassing!! That's my story & I'm sticking to it!! Off to Devon for Fri & Sat night in March hopefully will be able to get away from all the distractions & actually sleep!! So how are all those elephants doing over there??☺

This kept her laughing to herself for the rest of the evening and she couldn't wait to get some quiet time to reply. Having had a late night and early morning start Demi was able to offer a good reason to excuse herself early from her hosts and take herself off to her room. This gave her time to reply to Josh before falling asleep.

Men!! They'll do anything to attract attention & make out the ladies are doing the chasing!!☺ Just about over the hangover from last night & already in bed with my book as have an early start tomorrow. Jenny has booked us in for a spa day & treatments while we're in Durban as well as loads of other activities (hopefully not involving any rivers!!)☺ What have you got on this week? D☺

It wasn't long before he replied although Demi was already asleep and didn't see it until early the next morning. They were due to be flying to Durban and had to be at the airport by 6am.

Hectic week for me....Bingo with the ladies from the local bank branch on Thursday!!! Don't say a word.... I can't believe I let them talk me into it!!☺ Saturday night 1/4ly School boy's reunion down town!!! Enjoy your spa!☺

It was Wednesday and Jenny, Demi and Jenny's Mum Sue were out sightseeing around Durban. They had decided to head for the beach and cocktails. In the car, listening to the radio the DJ was talking about double whammy Wednesday and this reminded Demi of the text she had sent to Josh about 'hump day'. Thinking of this, while sitting back, relaxing in the car, gave Demi the perfect reason to text Josh.

They're talking of it being double-whammy Wednesday in SA today!? Not sure what it means!!?.?☺ Sounds like a good excuse to celebrate though so off to the Oyster Box (where Prince Albert of Monaco got married) for cocktails!!☺☺

Demi wasn't sure if she would get a reply as it was mid-week and not a usual time for them to be in contact. Just as she arrived at the Oyster Box Hotel she was elated to hear the signal from her phone indicating his reply. Oh how she wished he was with her in person. Her Prince Albert, in such a beautiful place. Maybe she could bring him here one day?

Hey u sounds like you're having an epic time....Don't hear much about the gym!!! Make the most of your last week!!☺

Demi had a fabulous time in Durban with Jenny and Sue. All too soon though she and Jenny were flying back to Jo'burg for a final couple of days.

Demi was just settled by the pool for some final sunshine when she received a text from Josh. Although it was Friday it was only the morning and, technically, her turn to text, so this was a lovely surprise.

Hey u not long left!! Hope you're topping up that tan to put the rest of us to shame!!☺

Demi sat up straight. Was this a sign that he was missing her and looking forward to her being back in the UK? Was he planning for them to meet? Demi was getting carried away with lovely dreamy thoughts. There was no better way to relax on a sunbed with fabulous thoughts of Josh being by her side very soon.

Allowing herself to dream about her beau and make virtual plans about their future, Demi took her time to self-indulge before replying.

Just catching the last few rays of sun before going back under winter wraps next week!! Have you got your dibber ready for tonight?!☺

She was pleased she remembered about his bingo and managed to get a 'flirty' innuendo in to her response.

Ohh do pay attention.☺ *Bingo was last night!!!*☺ *I didn't go as I was warned off...Apparently very scary little old ladies!!!*☺

Demi enjoyed his reply and went back with a chatty update.

Sunshine & cocktails make every day blend into one!!☺ *So is it School boy night then or is that tomorrow?? We are having a braai (SA for BBQ) tonight & then out at the crack of dawn tomorrow for a final game drive & to chase some more Ellies. D*☺

And that was it. No more holiday texts and no more holiday.

CHAPTER TWENTY FOUR
Decisions, Decisions

DEMI ARRIVED AT Heathrow in the early morning of 28th February. Feeling very cold and lonely, having gone from being with close friends around her 24/7 to having no-one, other than strangers, to speak to.

Stood at Heathrow waiting for her coach to take her back home Demi was lost in thought about Josh. She hadn't heard from him for a couple of days and after all his lovely texts she wondered what had changed. Was he now scared that she was back in the UK? Was he going to back off and become illusive? She had felt and hoped that they had got so much closer recently.

Demi was having a really bad sense about what the next few weeks would hold. Before her holiday Demi hadn't given much thought to life after it except that she hoped it would include Josh.

Lost in thought Demi hadn't noticed a man approaching. He stopped next to her and very nicely told her how beautiful she was and how lucky her boyfriend was to have someone like her. Taken aback, Demi managed to thank him and smile. Then, as what he said dawned on her Demi realised the tears running down her face. Feeling desperately alone, she wished Josh could hear what this man had said and she wished that he was with her now.

If only Demi knew what Josh was going through and how he was dealing with his emotions she would definitely have felt differently. Josh was struggling to come to terms with his feelings and having done so in the last 48 hours was now planning what to do next and how and when to put a plan into action. As yet he didn't have a plan and fear was preventing him from being decisive, something that he was not used to.

Demi arrived back at her home around mid-day and began to unpack and sort things out. She phoned her family to let them know she was back safely and slowly the loneliness lifted. She reminded herself how grateful she was for her family and friends and everything that she had. She was even beginning to look forward to going back to work the next day. Although she was suppressing the nagging worry that she had about what had happened while she had been away.

Later that afternoon Demi had a call from the Director. A little surprised by it Demi didn't really mind as obviously they were busy and it would be good to get a bit of an update before facing it full on.

As the conversation unfolded Demi began to realise that all was not good. Demi was told that a lot had changed while she had been away and that the Director wanted to meet Demi before Demi went back to the office. She went on to say that as she wouldn't be in the next day (Wednesday) that Demi should report to the Director's office at 9am on Thursday and that another one of the Executive Directors would also be at the meeting.

Demi asked if all was ok and if the Director could give Demi more information. Demi was told 'no' and that she would be told what she needed to know on Thursday at the meeting. Demi immediately knew something was very wrong. And what a very difficult and nasty person this Director was.

It was the next day before Demi received a text from Josh. With all the worry about work she had almost forgotten about him, having written him off as not wanting to be in contact anymore. In any event with what was about to happen to her he wouldn't want to know her anymore as it would disgrace his reputation to be associated with someone like she was about to become.

Hey u did you get back safely??☺

Josh could hardly contain himself. He had made his plan and couldn't wait to execute it. First he wanted to make sure that Demi was back in the UK and settling into normality. He wanted to give her that space for a couple of days as his plans would ensure that normality would definitely be very different for both of them.

Demi replied, doing her best to be cheery and not wanting to encourage him.

Hi. Yes thank you (unfortunately!☹) Adjusting to UK weather & lack of alcohol in the bloodstream isn't much fun!!☺

It's called detoxing!! Glad you're back in one piece.☺

Oh how she loved him and how she wanted things to be different. How could she possibly lead him on now? His work and reputation were important to him; as they were to Demi. He would never want to have someone in his network who would damage his credibility and that was what it would become if he got any closer to Demi and she wasn't going to let that happen.

The next day at the meeting at work Demi's world completely fell apart.

Having heard nothing further from Josh and not knowing how she could face him or even text him she decided that she had to end it now, before it had really started.

Meanwhile Josh had decided to get a grip of things. He could sense that he would have to be the gentleman and make the first move in getting them together. He now knew his reluctance; he had not wanted to ruin their friendship. Now though he realised that by not wanting to ruin their friendship he was stopping them from the potential of a beautiful relationship. After all, he knew he had fallen in love with the women behind the texts and he wanted to know if could fall in love with the women in front of the texts.

It wasn't as if Demi hadn't dropped him enough hints about how she felt and about meeting up. He had just been too 'male' to spot it at the time. Excitedly, he had been drafting and re-drafting an appropriate text to send to Demi. He couldn't decide between a day time coffee or an evening drink. Maybe he should go all out with a dinner invitation? He was in a real pickle. He had read and re-read Demi's texts to see if they helped and he just got himself in to more of a state. He needed to calm down.

He had a meeting to go to so he decided to go to it to take his mind off things and then to come back and make a final decision. Gosh, he really felt nervous; as if it was the first time he had done anything like this. It really felt very strange and nothing like he had experienced in a very long time.

He could not concentrate. The meeting was going on around him as if he was in a bubble. All he could think about was Demi and the text he was going to send her. He knew he would have to 'man up' and go with his gut instincts, although with too much effort gone into thinking he didn't know what his gut instincts were anymore.

After the meeting he decided to take some air. Maybe a quick walk and change of scene would help to clear his head. He walked through the office, talking to some of the staff on his way, out of the door and up the street to the coffee shop. He ordered a large take away double shot skinny latte and then slowly walked back.

That had been the tonic he needed. Back at his desk he decided to go for inviting Demi to coffee in the afternoon. That way, if all went well, they could do all 3. Coffee, followed by a glass of wine, followed by dinner. If things didn't go well then .... For him that wasn't going to happen and he loved his idea of setting up for all 3 to potentially flow from each other.

With this decision made he set about finalising his draft text. He then decided to wait until their usual Friday texting time to send his text now that he had finalised the wording. He was terribly excited and very nervous. Waking really early Friday morning he headed straight to the office to busy himself. He hoped that this would help the day go faster and that lunchtime would arrive quickly so that he could make his move.

Despite his nerves he was in a very upbeat mood. He had the text drafted in readiness so that all he had to do was press 'send' at the appropriate time. He had decided that lunchtime would be good as it wasn't too early and not too late for Demi to be able to see it, reflect, reply and get ready to meet up.

As 12 noon arrived Josh headed back to his office, retrieved his phone and scrolled to his draft text. Re-reading to check it, again, he was about to press 'send' when his phone 'pinged' with an arriving text. He wondered if it would be from Demi. If it was he would reply with his plan. Excitedly he opened her text.

Dear Josh, I have really enjoyed our texting friendship over the last few months & it is with great reluctance that I feel that I must ask you to stop texting me. Please make sure you put your divorce issues behind you & get that New You out there asap. Enjoy your Devon cottage weekend & I wish you every success & happiness in life & love. Look after those 2 daughters of yours – they sound very special. Take care & have loads of fun & thank you for your friendship. Demi

If Demi had known what Josh was planning she may have thought differently about ending their friendship.

* * *

PART TWO

CHAPTER TWENTY FIVE
Josh's Story – 'If Only'

ONE WEEK AFTER receiving Demi's 'end it all' text Josh was still disappointed. No, Josh was very disappointed, he realised as he sat reflecting over the last few weeks. Thirty five thousand feet in the air, quietly sitting in first class, he had time to sit back and think. And it was forcing him to re-run the last few weeks of his life.

He was on a long haul flight to a glorious holiday destination for some well-earnt and needed rest and relaxation. Although, he was beginning to regret having booked three weeks off if he was going to spend the whole time wallowing in self-pity and remorse.

If only he had sent his text to Demi when he had drafted it instead of waiting until the Friday. Why had he been so stupid? He was sorry for what could have been and wondered how good he and Demi would have been together.

If only he had come to his senses sooner instead of holding back and not allowing himself to see what was right in front of him. It's not as if Demi hadn't dropped him enough hints. He smiled as he remembered some of the fun banter they'd had. As he smiled he warmed at the closeness he felt to her. Why had he not seen this at the time? Why had he left it too late? What was Demi going through? It must be bad for her to have ended their relationship – such as it was.

Maybe that was it; she was fed up with waiting for him and had decided to move on with her life. If only she had given him a couple more days things would have been so different. For a start he wouldn't be jetting off long haul on his own, only now admitting to himself that he was using the excuse of a holiday to run away from his emotions.

Although, he was beginning to realise that rather than running away his mind and emotions were having different ideas and his time alone, away from everything and everyone, was going to be a time for him to re-evaluate his life and think about his future, whether he liked it or not. It was something that he knew needed to happen and yet something that he had been ignoring for a long time. Suddenly he felt scared and very alone. Would his 'holiday' be a good thing? He hoped so, despite how painful it was already feeling.

In Josh's need to get away from it all he had purposefully left his mobile phone behind. He had agreed with a few select people, his daughters, his boss and his best friend, that he would purchase a cheap 'pay as you go' phone so that he could be contacted in an emergency. He had also left them the details of where he was staying. This meant that he would have very limited contact with the rest of the world. This had seemed like a good idea at the time. Now he wasn't so sure.

If only he had taken his other mobile with him he would have been able to check it regularly to see if Demi had sent him a text. Not that he really had expected her to. She had made it very clear that she didn't want any contact with him. He hadn't even taken her number with him, which meant that he wouldn't be able to contact her, if he decided he wanted to, either. He really hadn't thought it through properly, had he?

It took Josh several days to settle in to his holiday destination and begin to relax. Each day he had been tempted to get the next flight back home. Luckily he didn't do that as when he started to relax he began to realise just how screwed up he had been over the last couple of years. He had immersed himself in work, he reflected, so as to hide away from the pressures of home and life in general.

Over the next few days he was able to re-live the last couple of years and he started to understand what had been happening. That turned out to be the best form of recovery as he was able to compartmentalise his life and understand it for what it was.

He could see where he had made some mistakes, what had made him feel guilty and the efforts he had made to keep things going. Yes, forgiveness was needed, and the valuable time away gave him the perfect opportunity to forgive those he needed to, and to understand why they had done what they had. More importantly he was able to forgive himself and he understood, with the beauty of hindsight, the whole situation. He had reviewed his life like watching a movie and had seen how all the characters had played their part and the intention and motives of their actions and behaviours.

By the beginning of his 3rd week Josh was able to start looking forward. To start to think about what he was going to do with the rest of his life having reflected on his job and career; his girls; his home; his hobbies; friends and social life.

Throughout all of his thoughts and reflections there had been one emotion that had remained; one emotion that he hadn't been able to shake off. It was still with him during his 3rd week and it became a stronger, more prevalent emotion and something that unless he gave it the time it was demanding, would not go away. In fact, he wasn't sure that he had wanted it to go away, which is perhaps why it remained, nagging him.

CHAPTER TWENTY SIX
Owed an Explanation

DEMI HAD HIT rock bottom and her world was shattered. Her work, reputation and status were incredibly important to her. It wasn't until it had been snatched away did she realise just how much.

Neither did Demi realise until then just how strong she was in the face of real adversity. She had a level of resilience rarely found. Having hit rock bottom Demi was determined not to stay there and to find the quickest way out and up. And with the support of her family and friends anything and everything was possible.

Throughout those few dark days Demi continued to think about Josh. She hadn't heard anything from him. Not that she expected to, after all she had told him not to contact her. Why then was she hurting so much and still letting him constantly fill her thoughts? How was he? How had he received her text? What was he thinking? Was he as upset as she was? Would he reply if she dared to text him again? Would she text him again? Could she text him again?

After several days of internal debate and lunch with Dyna, who was always sensible, Demi decided that nothing ventured, nothing gained. In any event, Josh need not reply if he didn't want to.

Choosing a Friday evening, three weeks after her 'end-it-all' text and pouring a large glass of wine for courage, Demi worked at creating the right words to send. Should she keep it short, just a quick 'how are you' or should she give an explanation?

She decided, under the circumstances, that she owed him an explanation.

PLEASE READ.....On my return from holiday I was presented with a serious work situation that I found difficult to deal with initially. My reaction to this prompted my last text to you. The situation, whilst serious also provides a number of opportunities that I am keeping optimistic & positive about – nothing much keeps me down for long and there is always something good that comes from everything if you look for it – This was just a tough one for me to get my head around for a few days. I am sorry that I did not tell you this before and for making the assumption that I should end our friendship as a result. I have really missed your texts and I would really like them to continue. I will understand though if you decide not to reply. I hope that you will at least accept my apology for the abruptness of my last text and that you might understand a little about what was behind it. Thank you for reading. Take care and best wishes. D

She just had to wait for his reply, if indeed he was ever going to. Being a Friday she had no idea whether he would be out and unable to reply or whether he would be at home and choosing not to reply. She knew she would have to wait, she just didn't know how long. She, of course, had no idea that Josh was two weeks into a 3 week holiday without his phone.

After waiting all week and through the next weekend with nothing from him Demi was convinced she would hear no more. Yes, she was very upset, only she didn't blame him. After all she had ended it abruptly and he was probably hurt by that, either that or he didn't care. Demi didn't really believe that he didn't care. She believed he did care and probably had so much going on in his life that he didn't need another emotional female complicating it.

Demi decided to put any hope of hearing from Josh behind her. She had plenty going on anyway at that time and needed to concentrate on putting her life back together. She had lots of decisions to make and a clear head would help her with that.

CHAPTER TWENTY SEVEN
Glad all Over

IT WAS MONDAY morning, four weeks after that fateful Friday when Demi had sent that 'end it all' text to Josh, and Demi had a busy day planned. Starting with the gym at 6.30am followed by a meeting with her solicitor and then some shopping for birthday presents. Demi stopped for coffee mid-afternoon to log into her phone and check emails. It was when she pulled her phone out she noticed she had a text message that she hadn't heard come through. Opening it, Demi felt scrummy inside. Wow, she hadn't expected that! Especially on a Monday morning!

Hi. Hope your work issues are getting better.☺

It took Demi a while before she replied. Her emotions were mixed and she wasn't sure what to expect. She read Josh's text over and over again. It was just a few words only they were potentially saying so much. There was no question for her to answer or prompting a response from her. There was a smiley, indicating that he was perhaps offering a friendly olive branch. After much deliberation Demi decided that it would be rude not to reply and that she would keep it short. She would wait until later though so that she could give it more thought.

Monday evening:
Hi. They are much better thank you. D☺

Almost straight away:
I'm glad.☺

Well, she definitely hadn't expected that! Now what should she do? Had he any idea what a turmoil he had put her in? Demi felt unable to respond as again there was no question, just a statement of fact. He sure wasn't making this easy.

Demi decided to 'play it cool' and to hold off responding. She had a busy couple of days ahead and they needed her concentration.

Over the next couple of days, try as she might, Demi could not get Josh out of her mind. She kept thinking about his last text "I'm glad.☺" and wondering just 'how glad' he was. The more she thought about it the more a song lyric jumped into her head and she found herself singing it over and over. Each time she did, she realised how happy it made her feel.

"Boom, boom, glad all over;
Yes I'm, Boom boom, glad all over;
I'm glad you're mine, all mine."

As Demi repeated the words their meaning and message dawned on her and she realised how apt they were. She wanted to share this with Josh to see if he picked up on it. Feeling playful Demi decided to text Josh to test him out on his 1960's 'pop' knowledge.

Thursday evening:
So, on a scale of 1-5 are you just 'glad' or are you a 'Dave Clark 5'?☺

Now she would have to wait to see if he would reply, first, and second, to see if he got the humour and reference.

And when she did get his reply it really made her laugh. She was also delighted to receive a 'chatty' text that was more than one line. Was it a sign of forgiveness? Would they be able to get their relationship back on track? Or was he just being kind to a friend in need?

Err I think I'm a retard?? Don't get it!! Do I need to ask a teenager?? Have 2 daughters now living with me in my 1 bed flat (long sad story!!) But all I can tell you is that I'm surrounded by bras, nickers & hormones... Ohh and my tellys been commandeered!!   On a serious note I'm glad, happy, elated (I haven't got a dictionary so can't look up anymore!!) that things have worked out ok!!☺

Needing time to think about how she felt and what Josh had said Demi held off responding. She also wanted to 'play it cool' and not crowd him out. It was still mid-week and he was undoubtedly busy. Tomorrow was Friday, so Demi would wait until then to reply.

Sounds like a blissful domestic nightmare – and makes me glad that I had boys!!☺ Dave Clark 5 was a band in the 60s who had a hit with 'Glad all Over' – obviously I learnt this from my Mum!!☺ Enjoy the lingerie.☺

Then came the test. Would he reply and if so when? She had kept her text as an answer only giving him no reason to need to reply if he didn't want to. Demi was pleased that she didn't have to wait long before getting her answer.

Ahh I thought that....!!☺ See I knew I shouldn't have just stuck with 80's greatest hits cd's.....There is more to life!!!!☺

Wondering if they would keep up a chatty rapport over the weekend, Demi didn't leave it too long before replying and took a risk with popping in a frisky twist that she hoped wouldn't scare him off.

Clearly you've led a sheltered life & have a lot to learn & experience!! Make sure you find the right tour guide!☺

And that was it. Nothing, Demi had no idea what sort of weekend Josh had planned, whether he was working or had time off. She no longer felt the same part in his life in the way that she had before they split. Although, with the way that she had treated him and let him down, she couldn't really expect anything else. Would he ever trust her again?

Demi felt even sorrier for herself, alone, sad and wondered why her life had changed so dramatically over the last few weeks. What had she done to deserve that?

Usually Demi was quite resilient and bounced back from any knocks quickly. She could always forgive, see the positives and move on. This time though she just couldn't shake it off and get herself there. She could feel herself spiralling lower and lower, completely shattered by what had happened and the way she had been treated. Demi knew that she had to end these feelings and the burden of recent events affecting her and her family.

CHAPTER TWENTY EIGHT
Miracle

T HE NEXT FEW days turned out to be the most difficult for Demi and her family. They now understood how lives could be so dramatically changed in just a couple of seconds. The lorry had just come from nowhere, the car was completely smashed and how anyone had survived was a miracle in itself.

It was Sunday evening, a week later and all was quiet when Demi's phone 'pinged' with a text having come through. On opening it, it was from Josh and a long chatty update, woven with his own dilemmas and sadness.

Hey u – this week has been a bit different!! Was thinking about texting you but I always seem to pass on my woos so thought I would save you from it.... Just in case you thought I'd won the chocolate brownie!! I mentioned before that both girls were now living with me in my 1 bed 1 box room town house! Well it all got too much for my eldest daughter who attempted to take an overdose this week and we ended up at A&E for a night!! Then I had to give a presentation to 100 kids the next day. Both gigs were frightening!! Just sorting some counselling to help pick up the pieces for the girls as pretty busted up after years of emotional turmoil!! Anyway who'd be a dad!! Just got a 3 bedroom rental booked for 4 weeks' time... Ohh what I'd give to see a radiator again that didn't have knickers and bras drying on it!!☺

How would Demi respond to this? She felt as if she should go back with an attempt to lift his spirits. She owed him this at least, after all he had no idea what her family had been going through and clearly relied on her for a little bit of support and light relief.

And how are you? It sounds like you're having a real nightmare and I wish your daughters all the best on their steps forward. Please don't worry about sharing your woos with me - I'm used to it from plenty of others and I'm a good listener. If there is anything I can do feel free to ask. After all, they say that 1 problem shared is a problem halved!! I'm off work at the moment so have plenty of spare time. The new 3 bed rental sounds like a good move - excuse the pun!!☺ Take care and feel free to share any time.☺

She hadn't expected the question that followed. On reflection she would have to be more careful with the content of her texts so that she could anticipate what Josh might ask or want to know.

How come you're off work???☺

Deciding to go with a light hearted response, with some humour in the hope of keeping both of their spirits up. She had been enjoying the conversation so far and was looking forward to building their relationship. Some day she would tell Josh the full story. Not just yet though, as she felt that neither of them was ready for it.

Oh dear! That's a really difficult question for me to answer save to say that there will be a happy ending. In the meantime you might have to share the chocolate brownies!!☺

Not expecting another text as it was getting late, and Demi would usually be going to bed at this time, she put the phone down and settled into attempting to get some sleep.

However, Josh clearly wanted to keep chatting, as the next morning there was a response that made her smile.

I'll get a packet in!!! I hope on the Dave Clarke 5 glad all over index (hope I've got your retro pop group right!!!) that everything works out ok.☺

She wondered if she should reply now or whether to wait until Friday. Deciding to respond that day, just later on, as she had busy plans first thing, and then it would be over to Josh to respond, which she guessed would not arrive until at least Friday.

Thank you. It will. Well done for the retro link!☺ Hope you have a better week this week and remember to let me know if there is anything I can do.☺

Friday came and went with nothing from Josh to stop the wondering if his week had been better and a little more settled or whether there had been more turmoil. If she hadn't heard from him soon she would have to text him to find out. As she had a busy Saturday planned she hadn't wanted to wait all day, or miss a text if Josh decided to make contact later, so she decided to make the first move.

Hi. How's your week been? I've just finished some painting so feeling a bit 'chuffed' with myself!☺ I'm off to an indoor picnic this afternoon as part of an 18th birthday weekend of parties & surprises. What are you up to?☺

She laughed at his reply.

I'm at Macro ahhhhh..... Will send you war and peace when I find the escape hatch.☺

She would be warmed by this for the rest of the day, even if he did forget to send 'war and peace' later.

Then, as promised, Josh sent a more chatty text that would bring Demi into his confidence again. She loved and appreciated the closeness and intimacy of their relationship, even if it was just over universal wave lengths. Their banter and respect was closer than most married couples. Somehow she would have to find a way to bring them together, in person.

She knew that would have to wait a while yet as neither of them were emotionally ready and she wasn't sure how either of them would cope with it either at that time.

War and Peace:

Hi u – if I remember correctly you were painting not so long ago!! Should I worry about solvent abuse??? You can get help.☺ Well sat outside our new rental on a local 'reservation'!! The girls have been asking me loads of questions about what the house has and hasn't got....Well I did the blokes look around... Where does the telly go!! Just been looking for a washing machine... How the mighty fall!!☺

I've got to get some kicks from somewhere!! Where's the fun in living the life of a saint all of the time!!☺ A tumble dryer might also be a good idea as it will save you from the bras & knickers!☺ With every negative there is an opposite reaction therefore after a fall there must be a rise – how exciting is that!!☺☺

Hey you might be right there philosopher.☺ I'm off to buy a plunger after the girls hair has blocked up the sink....Did you mean the rise and fall in the water levels???☺ Neither girls were that impressed with my choice of house... May have been all the cars up on bricks I guess??? Can't all be changing their winter tyres over this weekend surely??☺

Mr Muscle sink unblocker is a good purchase for hair clogging the plug holes!! Trust me as I have to use it regularly!☺ I'm not sure how impressed I would be if I was moving into a wigwam (link to reservation!) in this weather either!!☺☺ I've managed to escape the evening party as all the youngsters have gone out on the razz. So I'm back home with cocoa & sleepers & the excitement of Britain's Got Talent to look forward to!!☺

That had been a fun day of texting, and she could sense the closeness of their friendship. Sunday was a new day to look forward to. Would the texting continue? Having more birthday celebrations to organise and attend would keep her busy all day Sunday anyway. Demi was being taken care of and had plenty to keep her occupied. If the texting didn't flow that day it wouldn't have too much of an impact other than she would be wishing that he could be joining in with their day of fun.

Josh was first to text, which helped to kick the day off to a good start.

Hey old timer... Fancy giving up on a party! Do they still play the 'funky chicken' song?? Thanks for the tip on Mr muscle!! I went with a few friends for an Indian last night... being half Indian one would have thought I'd have been conditioned... However I think I'll have a day indoors today and not venture too far!!!☺☺

She got the sense that Josh would at least be safe that day and hopefully he would stay close to home, particularly if he was feeling a bit delicate. She kept her reply to the point and not too chatty, she realised with reflection, when she hadn't heard from him again by the evening. She hoped he was feeling better.

Who are you calling 'old timer'?? Pot, kettle and black seem to come to mind!!☺ Especially with a reference to the 'funky chicken' song!!!! Sorry to hear about the unconditioned Indian!!!! At least the weather is conducive with a day indoors. Not sure what my plans are yet. I'm either putting the room back straight after finishing the painting and/or going out for more birthday celebrations. Have a good day.☺

CHAPTER TWENTY NINE
Paint Fumes

JAINI HAD A challenging week ahead, with the big part of it being spent with Demi. There had been no response from Josh since Sunday and if something new came in that week it would be a surprise as it would break the normal weekend pattern. Therefore, when she did receive a text in amongst the busyness of the week, and a long chatty one at that, she was delighted.

Hey u – How's tricks? Still sniffing those paint fumes?? Been busy since both my girls started living with me in my bachelor pad! Have rotas for everything!! Haven't seen myself in the bathroom mirror for days as it's been steamed up with constant baths etc... When I do finally get to see myself I'm guessing I'll be a lot greyer!! Anyway have the bigger rental from the end of this month so should be able to get into my own bathroom at least once a week!! Speaking of which I've booked a slot for the bathroom for tomorrow night as I'm on a night out down town with some of my old school palls!! Probably be left feeling even older by the end of the night!!☺

What was his real message here? Was he telling Demi about his night out in the hope that she would be there? As tempting as that was Demi would most definitely not fall into that trap. After all, that would be something close to stalking, which was definitely not Demi's style at all.

Anyway, she was going away that weekend, so it seemed a good opportunity to let Josh know this in her reply. She hoped it wouldn't stop him from texting, only she had a feeling it might. She had thought about cancelling her weekend plans as her sister needed her. The children had told her to keep with her plans and that a weekend away would do her good. They would make sure that they looked after her sister.

Hi – all good with me thanks. What will 'even older' say about that!! Maybe you should go for her sister 'slightly younger' instead!!☺ You could always say you're going for the distinguished Matt le Blanc look – how gorgeous is he?? – not that I've been looking obviously!!☺ I'm off to Bristol early Saturday morning to visit my cousins. We are going to pop to Cardiff for some shopping & then I'll come back on Sunday. I bet you can't wait until the end of the month. The move will be really exciting for you all. Have fun tomorrow night & good luck with getting your bathroom slot!!☺☺

Keeping her resolve, as Demi had done, in not chasing Josh seemed to be working as Josh appeared keen to keep in touch and although there were a few long gaps in the week he had begun to text every few days. Was that a sign that he was allowing himself to get closer to Demi.

She hadn't told him about the accident yet. She didn't really know why. Perhaps it was because it was still too difficult to talk about or perhaps she didn't want to add to his burden of worries. She would tell him soon.

It was the middle of the next week before Josh replied, however that was fine. He had obviously wanted to give her space to enjoy her weekend away and had gone for an early start.

Hey u how was your weekend in the south west?? I have a confession... I went saddo shopping, washing machine, toaster, microwave... beds etc!!! It was really boring!! Previously the extent of my shopping had been how big is the telly or how loud is the stereo!!! Boy what a shock this new life is!! Had burnt pizza topped off with oven cleaner (tried to oven pride as well this weekend!!) I will let you know if I survive!!☺

Early morning, particularly if Josh was on a train somewhere, she knew from previous texts, could be a good time to chat. Being hopeful, she went for a quick reply.

South West was great thanks. I'd forgotten how beautiful it was around there. I'm sure you'll soon be back to shopping for your designer jeans. In the meantime go steady on the oven cleaner as one product can lead to another and before you know it you'll be on the paint fumes!!!☺ I could say 'Happy Hump Day' only I don't want you to get the wrong idea again!!☺

Being a Wednesday and 'hump day' reminded her of the texts they had sent each other when Demi was in South Africa. A time when everything had seemed so simple in comparison to how it was now. Oh how life had changed in just a few weeks.

Josh, obviously keen not to disappoint, was equally quick to respond.

Hey u – you're sounding perkier which is good to hear!! By that I don't mean as in Pinky and Perky... Not that I'm old enough to remember them!!! I'm on the Cross Country train service to Manchester...Everyone is double booked tired and grumpy... Boy do I know what national hump day is now!!! Mind you I do prefer the version I remember from my courting days!!!☺

That made her laugh and pleased that he was in a good mood and in a fun place. She had also been correct on guessing that he was sat, bored, on a train. She loved the reference to hump day and he clearly remembered the fun they'd had weeks before. If only he knew what had changed and by how much. Would he still be smiling then? She hoped he would once he got over the initial shock.

It was a short while later before she was able to reply as she had been busy and needed to get a couple of emails sent before she could allow herself time to enjoy that special moment with Josh. Demi had always loved this sort of time. When it felt like there was no-one else, apart from them, in the world.

I will do my best to ignore the association you have made with me and pigs and will focus on the fact that they were cute and fun!!!☺ You might want to keep the vision of your version with you for the rest of the day – just be careful you're not the only one smiling as you may get some weird looks!!☺

His reply warmed her and she knew that was where to leave it for that day. She would save her turn to text for tomorrow.

Smiling already – thank you!☺

CHAPTER THIRTY
Exaggerated Fun

T HE REST OF THE day would be spent at the hospital visiting her sister. At least she was now on the mend and the worst was over. Demi and Jaini were very close, being only one year apart in age they had grown up together and were each other's best friends as well as close sisters and second Mum's to each other's children.

The past couple of weeks had been very challenging for the whole family. Demi and Jaini's children had been brilliant in the way they had been coping and helping out. However, emotionally they were all still in shock as nothing on this level of seriousness had ever affected the family as this had done and would continue to do.

The hospital and nursing staff were fantastic in their support and care. Without their kindness things would have been far more difficult to cope with. Today was going to be a special day and would be a telling day on the next level of recovery that could be expected. Today was the day when her sister would be helped to stand and begin a long journey to get her legs working again following that horrific accident that had changed all their lives in the blink of an eye.

This was going to be Demi's biggest challenge yet. She had debated long and hard whether to share this with Josh and had decided that he was too fragile. Instead she had been determined to protect him and keep to providing a non-needy friend who gave him support to get his life back on track.

Demi had done a good job of this over the last few months and it was something she was determined to continue and to maintain their relationship. In time she would tell him and this would be when both he and Demi were emotionally strong enough to deal with it. In the meantime she had her sister's long term wellbeing to concentrate on.

Back home after her hospital visit there was just enough time to bake some cakes in preparation for Demi's niece, Cesca's baby shower that she was going to tomorrow. When she had finished she decided to text Josh to tell him what she had been up to. After all it was Friday and time for the usual weekend chatter.

What is the world coming to eh?? I've just spent the afternoon baking cakes and I was so sure that I was destined for so much more!!!!☺ However, the good thing with no-one else being around was that I got to have the spoons, spatulas and bowls all to myself......Yummy!!! It was the best 15 minutes (to coin a phrase!!) of pleasure I've had in a long time!!!!☺☺

She wondered how he would take her innuendo and whether he would continue the fun. She was delighted when he replied and she laughed out loud. She loved the way he always managed to bring his 'grumpy old man' bit into the fun.

That much fun with your clothes on??? I don't believe you!! Just had my own version of fun... 6 hours on a Virgin Cross Country train back from Manchester!!! Do you have to be rude to work for the train companies or do you think they send them on a course to train them up specially???☺ PS save me some cake!!☺

And she couldn't resist her reply and equally enjoyed his quick response.

6 hours?? And on a virgin!!?? Puts my 15 minutes to shame!!☺

Cheeky!! Don't believe everything you hear... Us guys are known to exaggerate!!!☺

The baby shower was great fun and the first one she had ever been too. They weren't around when it was her turn to have babies. Cesca received some lovely presents and it was a pleasure seeing a room full of young ladies having so much fun and laughter without the need for alcohol. They were a good example of restoring faith in young people that anyone would have had the pleasure to witness. As it was her turn to text she thought she would use the excuse of the baby shower to update him on her weekend adventures and to find out what he had been up to.

Hey, how was your Friday? I went to a baby shower last night which was lovely – hence the cake making!!☺ Have you anymore 'domestic' shopping to do this weekend or have you a more relaxed time planned??? I haven't decided what to do yet as was waiting to see what the weather was like and as the sun is shining I might take advantage of it. Other plans are to start decorating another room!!!!! Thank goodness for the sunshine!!!☺ Have fun!☺

His reply showed an element of frustration and stress although she felt that he was dealing with it well. There was also a good balance of family time. It would be good to see him settled in his new accommodation with his new domestic arrangements.

Hi u yesterday was crap!! Hit the ironing hard last night... Those shirts got a steaming and a half!!! Went for a lovely run on the beach at 5ish this morning... Just been to sign our new lease and the girls and I are off to have a celebratory breakfast!!! Then joy of joy, off to the shops with them to buy more cack stuff for the house!! So you didn't save me any cakes then?? Are you sure you didn't eat them all??☺

She replied, wishing him a fun day.

Hi. Sorry to hear yesterday was horrid!! Good news today though with the lease signing. Enjoy breakfast & the shops – lucky you!! Have still got some chocolate ones left only you'll have to be quick because as soon as my lot see them they'll be gone!! Have a fun day!!☺

There was no reply from Josh and she wondered when it might come. Her week was busy. Her sister was making excellent progress although she wanted more, more quickly, for both of them.

Demi was worried about her sister. She was looking tired and yet she was still managing to show everyone love and support. Demi was worried that Jaini was more concerned about others and not concentrating on herself as much as she should be and needed to be. Demi would make sure she spoke to her boys and nieces to see if there was any more they could do to help. Clearly Cesca was limited with what she could do and at least a new baby would bring the family, especially Jaini, something to celebrate and enjoy. Demi would do her best to make sure Jaini had opportunity to spend as much time as possible with her new grandchild.

CHAPTER THIRTY ONE
Funky Chicken

THE EXCELLENT PROGRESS her sister had made meant that she had been able to begin walking with crutches, albeit slowly, and she had managed to stand unsupported for quite a few seconds. The prognosis was good and the Doctors were sure that it wouldn't be too long before she would be back home walking unaided and resuming a normal life. This was great news and demonstrated her sister's strength and zest for life.

The accident had been horrific and the fact that she had survived was a miracle. The thought of being able to return to her previous self within a fairly short timeframe was almost beyond belief.

With so much going on she had not given Josh too much thought. When a text came through that morning she had not expected it to be from Josh. She was very excited when she saw that it was and enjoyed his humour.

Hi Delia how's your week been? I've been in London working for the IBSA for much of the week – managed to pick up a man cold so a grumpy Griswold today!! Got my long service award (£75 for 10yrs) from Grants Holding this week (wow!!!)... Spent it on toilet brushes and towels!! Boy where did all the fun go??? Actually think that's what's made me grumpy as would rather have blown it on some new designer gear!! Off to a friend of my mum's 80th tomorrow (boy am I selling myself)!! Guess it's going to be a lot of grannies dancing to the funky chicken song!!☺

She was at home, taking stock with a cup of coffee, so was able to set about constructing a reply. Not knowing that there was to be a fun couple of hours of banter that followed.

Hi. My week has been fairly busy with shopping for baby things, going to the gym and lots of coffee!!! You've probably got IBSA fever having been there most of the week – commonly known as Grumpy Old Nerd – have a hot toddy and a chocolate brownie (or 3!) and you'll be fine in no time!!☺ £75 is better than a smack in the eye and it wouldn't have given much towards new designer gear anyway!! Toilet brushes and towels are always useful items!!☺ You better get practicing your dance moves or those grannies will put you to shame!! ☺

Hey cheeky! What's all this baby shopping???? Surely you must be of an age whereby you can buy grown up clothes!!☺

Think it must be my new fetish – baby clothes are sooooo cute!! Becoming a Great Aunt probably sounds more suited to shopping for surgical stockings and incontinence pants. I wonder if they do a designer line in those outlet shops????☺

Lol – Ok, ok you've got me!!☺

Ok, so now my imagination has gone into overdrive wondering where, when, what and how I've got you!!!!☺☺

She was hoping for an equally 'flirty' reply and was slightly disappointed that his justification came across so seriously.

You had me speechless (textless) on the gear one can source from Outlet shops these days!!☺

She decided to push him some more.

Now I am really laughing, mostly with embarrassment, as clearly my attempts to 'flirt' have lost their mojo!!!☺☺ Things seem to get lost or misinterpreted in text translation!!!☺

She wondered whether her reply would make him run or whether he would have the nerve to front it out. It didn't take long before it was clear that he had backed off, again. What was he so scared of? Or maybe she was reading too much into it as he had mentioned that he had a cold. He could just be feeling too poorly to be bothered to text and was using the weekend to rest, which would definitely be good for him with everything he had been going through recently.

Not wanting to let the weekend go without more contact and wondering how long it would be before Josh replied she thought she would use his cold to find out how he was and whether he had made it to the funky chicken party.

Hey hope you're feeling better. How was your party yesterday? Did you escape the funky chicken??☺ I managed to paint the ceiling ready to embark on the walls today. This room is a bit more challenging than the others so it should keep me out of mischief for a while!!☺ Have a good day!☺

She didn't have to wait too long for his reply and was pleased to hear that he hadn't been too poorly to stop him from enjoying his weekend.

Hiya. I'm babysitting two 9 year old twins...Full of cold... And feeling the effects of too much chilli con carnie or orange juice yesterday!!! Just want to die quietly somewhere!!! Give me painting any day... Well smelling the fumes!! Did my good deed last night as the drunken couple from next door locked themselves out so I invited them in for coffee until midnight when their daughter came back!! Late one for me!!☺

Having embarked on more decorating and a slightly bigger project she was finding it tough going and used it as a base for her reply.

Phew!! This is hard work!! I'll swap you for the twins??!!☺ Sorry you're feeling so poorly, maybe a walk in the sunshine will help.☺ Well done for your good deed last night!! Hope you'll soon be feeling better.☺

Then all was quiet and she was back to a week of hospital visits, solicitors, and decorating. In the back of her mind was Josh's move date at the coming weekend, which she wanted to make sure she remembered so that she could send him her best wishes. So when Saturday morning arrived and, having not heard from Josh with his usual Friday text, she went for a quick one liner to wish him well.

Hi. Good luck with the move!! I hope it all goes well. Have fun!☺

Knowing he would be busy she didn't expect a reply anytime soon. In any event she was also busy and suffering from a hangover from a late night of fun with the family.

Thanks – been a nightmare!! Got to house to find they'd had a gas leak and the gas board were digging the drive up!! Never a dull moment!!☺

At least the sun is shining!! Does the TV look good??☺ I've had a slow day shaking off a combination of my first jaeger bomb, a rock band & my family from last night!!!☺ Hope you get your boxes sorted & find some time to enjoy the weather.☺

Hey you my 50 inch looks great!!! Even in my 60 inch lounge!!!☺

Wow!! I'm impressed!!☺

Taking advantage of an early night she didn't see Josh's response until the morning.

Sorry ill in bed will update you on the move when I'm back up and about!!

She was sorry to hear he was poorly again although not surprised with everything going on. She wished she could help him and wondered who he did have to offer him support at this time. He hadn't mentioned anything about any of his friends being around to help out. He also hadn't mentioned whether either of his girls were there and busy working along with him.

Not wanting to disturb him or put any pressure on she responded with a short text of support and sympathy.

Make sure you get some rest & drink lots of water. I hope you feel better soon. Take care!!

She couldn't help smiling when she read his reply and felt a gentle 'ticking' off was needed.

Thanks do you think you could ask the local church to tone the bells down please!!

Now you're just being plain grumpy!!☺

That obviously kept him quiet for a while and not expecting to hear anything more until Friday it was somewhat out of the blue when it was only Tuesday and an Executive Board day, when she heard from him.

Hi ya Board day so really busy with managing challenging adults... (I think!!) – Anyway just wanted to say thank u for listening to my woes and to let u know that I am feeling better after discovering man flu was food poisoning!!☺

It was at times like these that it was good that Demi wasn't with him. She didn't cope very well with nursing or cleaning up after illnesses involving body fluids. She text him back straight away to thank him and wish him well, knowing that he would be far too busy to text anymore today.

Oh dear, poor you! Good luck with Board day!! That's kind of you to let me know. I am pleased to hear you're feeling better!☺

This was definitely a week of lovely surprises as the next day, quite unexpectedly again, Josh was sending another 'early bird' text. She was slightly concerned that this man never seemed to stop, even when he was clearly not very well. He was still running the Executive Board day and chasing around the country with no sign of resting. Anyway, she was pleased that despite all of that, he was keeping in contact. She would make sure that she relished in it and enjoyed it for what it was.

Hi on 'location'... (sounds good ehh??)... In Melton Mowbray... Guess I've blown it by saying where!! Feeling stronger today although still being careful with what I eat and drink. I hope things are getting better for u too. I will be back in the office next week and hopefully will be back eating soon.☺

A bit of light banter followed.

Hi. Being on 'location' obviously suits you.☺ Shame you're not well enough to enjoy the pies!! Or will you make an exception & suffer the consequences??!!☺

I travelled light and so only have the one pair of boxers... Think I'll play safe and just stick to the bottled water!!☺

Under the circumstances bottled water is probably a good idea!!☺

It then went quiet although she didn't really notice for a couple of days as she herself was busy. There was a lot going on with still making regular visits to the hospital, decorating, and the new baby due any day now.

CHAPTER THIRTY TWO
Holding Back

U NDER THE CIRCUMSTANCES Demi was coping very well, training herself to keep focused on all the positive things in her life and being grateful for everything and everyone she had. Jaini was also keeping her spirits up and their daily time together in the hospital was always full of fun, laughter and encouragement for each other. She was making fabulous progress and was expected to be home around the same time the new baby was expected to arrive. The consultant just wanted to make sure she was stable and independent with the use of only one crutch. She was almost there.

Being so determined and strong minded had been the things that had kept her going. She had undergone the most gruelling physio regime and was now stronger and fitter than any of them. Her dream was to get back to running, even a short distance, and the Doctors couldn't see any reason why she wouldn't be able to do it, in time.

It would soon be time for Jaini to let Demi know what she had done. She wasn't too sure how Demi would react although hoped that after the initial shock she would be pleased and excited.

Having not heard from Josh over the weekend she hoped that it was because he was taking time out to rest and recover. With it being a bank holiday it would give him an extra day off. She felt that she needed to leave him to it and hoped he would text when he was ready and back in the land of the living.

It was Tuesday before Josh next text Demi and she was surprised that he had found the strength to have a weekend away. Although she was pleased that he had managed to recover and had used the bank holiday to full advantage with having at least one lazy day.

Hi how was your bank holiday weekend? Went to Torquay to see two sets of friends one of whom you might remember Rich Philips who worked with me at Insurance 4 U!! Was feeling sorry for myself yesterday (washed my favourite white designer tee shirt with my daughters sheets and it came out ready for a gay pride walk!! So had a really wasteful day... totally unlike me... Lay on the settee channel hopping for 7 hours!!! Truly ashamed of myself!!!☺

He did make her laugh – there was never a dull moment in his life. She wondered how he did it and managed to keep going. Without wanting to take advantage of his good nature she asked him if he could give any pointers on business start-up and pensions and popped a question into her reply.

She had been thinking ahead about a possible business that she and her sister could set up when she was out of hospital and feeling up to it. It was something that the sisters had spoken about before so it would be no surprise. The timing felt as if it might be right to do it now and maybe this could be the something positive to come out of all the heartache over the last couple of months.

Hey! My weekend was really busy!! I've decorated the lounge (& it looks fab!!) & I helped at a charity day on Sunday (& got freezing cold!!). Housework, banking, emails & various chores today to catch up!! I'm not sure I do remember Rich although his name is slightly familiar. Sometimes a lazy day on the sofa is just what is needed so don't beat yourself up too much – think of the rest you got & how much better you feel!!!☺ Sorry to hear about the designer tee!! Do you happen to know anything about setting up a business and/or setting up a private pension scheme?!?!! If so, please can I pick your brains some time – no rush?!?☺ Hope you have a good week.☺

And almost straight away Josh was on the case and wanting to find out how he could help.

Hey you royalist you!! I'm not an expert at business start-ups but do know a bit about a stakeholder pension scheme – how can I help?☺

Giving a quick explanation and a chance to not respond for a while, she was pleased he was straight on the case for her.

Thank you! Having always belonged to an employer's pension scheme if I left employment and set up a business I guess I need to set up a private pension scheme of some sort so my questions are – what sort of pension do I need & where do I go to get one? Please bear in mind that I know nothing about pensions!!☺ PS. There's no rush so please don't worry about getting straight back to me!! Thank you for any help you can give.☺

Despite her second reassurance of there being no rush, half an hour later Josh replied with all the information she needed to get started with. He truly loved his work and she now felt guilty for asking him and giving him something extra to do.

Hi obviously I can't give you advice under the financial regulations!!☺ However lots of people tend to go for a stakeholder pension scheme with an Insurance company or bank. I know an IFA who I really trust who is able to give advice! His name is George Booth and his no is 05323312304. I am sure George will give you some pointers if you want to call him and feel free to mention my name!!☺

It was good to have friends in the right places, although she felt a bit guilty at taking advantage. He didn't appear to mind though and had been very helpful.

Thank you. I appreciate the 'advice' position. This gives me a good starting place & I'll give George a call. Have fun!!☺

It was definitely understandable why Demi had fallen for this man. It was amazing how they had built such a close relationship just through texting. Wondering how she could encourage Josh to let his guard down and invite her to meet him, although she knew that right now wouldn't be a good time for either of them with everything going on in their lives. A new relationship needed time and dedication if it was going to stand any chance of long term survival.

Perhaps when her sister was out of hospital and life was more settled she would see what she could do to encourage things if they hadn't developed naturally by then. She was convinced that Josh was just as keen as she was, and that self-confidence was holding him back, was holding them both back.

CHAPTER THIRTY THREE
Grumps

IT WAS FRIDAY evening and feeling excited about going out with her friends she wanted to let Josh know about it. She hoped he would ask where she was going and that by some coincidence they may be going to a similar part of town.

WARNING... WARNING... WARNING... The She Monster is out on the town tonight!!!☺ Hi! How was your short week? I'm out with the girls tonight – wish me luck!! Not too much planned for this weekend. What are you up to?? Whatever it is have fun. D☺

The fantasy was soon dashed when Josh's reply didn't arrive until the next afternoon.

Hi you sorry just picked up your text!! Did you have a good time last night?? Had my friend round with her kids this morning...Her son peed on my wall!!! Then my mum called in...Trying to get washing and chores done with all these visitations is a nightmare... Don't they know I need to get things out on the line!!! Now I am getting like Victor Meldrew!!! I'm at the IBSA on Monday so need to get my outfit sorted to make sure I fit in!!☺

Wondering whether he sounded as if he was in a chatty mood she set about composing a comprehensive response.

Hi, I had a great time last night/early hours of this morning thanks!!! Fortunately I managed not to over indulge so feel better than expected today!!☺ I'm afraid that's boys for you!!! They have no scruples about when & where!!!☺ It sounds like you have been watching too many scary movies with all your visitations and nightmares.☺ It has felt a bit slow this week, probably due to the bank holiday, so hopefully things will pick up again next week. I hope you manage to get the washing dry – make sure you use lots of pegs or you could end up chasing your 'smalls' all around town!! And what would Victor have to say about that?.?!!☺

What followed was complete silence. She was disappointed to start with. Then as her week got underway she became too busy to worry about it.

And what a busy week! It was Demi's birthday Wednesday and arrangements were in place to meet for lunch and to have an afternoon outdoors. They were planning to go out of hospital for the afternoon too, which they were all very excited about.

There was only one thing that would change their plans and they were all on tender hooks. At 7.30am they got the call that they had half expected and that would completely change their plans. Demi's niece had gone into labour and baby was on its way. Demi's birthday lunch and afternoon out with Jaini would be postponed as birthing partner duties needed to be performed.

Josh hadn't known it was Demi's birthday so there had been no expectation for him to text mid-week. Josh's usual Friday text failed to arrive and as there was nothing from him Saturday morning either she decided she would have to break the silence. It had been an exciting week for Demi and she wanted to share just a little bit of it with him.

Hey u how's your week been? Mine has been good starting with buying tickets for the Silverstone F1 GP in July.☺ Then we had our new baby arrive on Wednesday, sharing her birthday with her great aunt!!☺ And finishing with England winning the football! All in all quite a good week!!☺ Got my cousin visiting tomorrow otherwise a quiet weekend. What about you??☺

She was beginning to worry about him and what possible dramas he could be going through when eventually his response 'pinged' through.

Hiya sorry had a really busy week. One day in London and a couple of days up North!!! Shattered... Well I'm an old boy now!! Had a really stressful week trying to hold the sale of the ex-matrimonial home together!!! Been sorting out the kids cars today. And then to top it all the gypsy wedding family next door had a karaoke sing along last night!!! So a quiet night of ironing beckons tonight!! Off to a National Trust Castle with my girls and adopted family tomorrow for father's day which should be nice!! Signed grumps!!!☺

He really was having a tough time. If only Demi could hold his hand or stand next to him, she knew that would help to make things easier for him. She understood why he wouldn't let anyone in, only she wished he would re-assess and relent, just a little bit.

Oh dear! We are feeling grumpy aren't we?.?!! (Understandably.) Just make sure Dopey & Sleepy don't get jealous!!☺ I hope you enjoy the National Trust Castle with the girls & adopted family.☺ ☺

Boy I'm definitely the one feeling old!! Just been watching Bewitched how sad is that for a Saturday night!!!☺ PS when will it be summer?.?☺

Fortunately Josh's text got lost in the ether and didn't arrive until later that evening. It was the next morning before she saw it and replied, which gave more chance for another day of contact. It was Father's Day and gave her an excuse to mention it.

Sorry for the late reply my phone signal is messing up and I didn't get your text until late last night!! Just be careful when you wriggle your nose – otherwise you might turn the cat into a rabbit!!☺ Summer starts today!!! Happy Father's Day!! So have a lovely time at the Castle – in the Summer Sunshine!!☺☺

She knew he would be up early and hoped he wouldn't take too long replying. And sure enough..............

Thanks.☺ All grumpy in my household this morning... Girls don't do early Sunday mornings!! Washed the car already, hung the washing on the line...Brought it back in again and hung it on the rails inside!! How does this father's day thing work?!!☺

I find lowering my expectations helps! It gives me less to be disappointed over and more to get excited about!!☺ Here endeth today's lesson!! Now relax and have fun!!☺

She hoped he would relax enough to enjoy his day. A brisk walk in the fresh air and sunshine was usually a good cure for any ill. Whether he showed it on the outside or not she was sure that deep down he would enjoy it, especially having his family and close friends with him.

Having her own Dad to visit, a new baby to cuddle and time at the hospital to fit in she was in for a busy day herself.

Demi was pleased to see Jaini when she visited the hospital. There was a lot to catch up on and photos of the new baby to share. They had a fun time and with the nice weather they were able to go outside for a while. It was great, and the highlight of the day was watching her sister take her first steps outside. Her progress was phenomenal and the Doctors were sure she would be home very soon and leading a normal life again within the next couple of months.

There were a few small adjustments at home that were needed to help out in the short term and she would get the boys in the family on to this over the next few days. She didn't want her sister having to spend time in hospital she didn't need too, despite understanding the challenges they would all face when she came home. The saving point for this was knowing that it would be short term recovery time only - and it could have been so much worse.

CHAPTER THIRTY FOUR
Football Crazy

DEMI WAS OPTIMISTIC and very excited about the 'home coming'. Jaini was also excited only she had a big decision to make and this worried her a bit and marred some of the excitement as she wasn't sure how Demi would react when she told her.

These thoughts and plans filled Demi's mind over the next couple of days. Not expecting to hear anything from Josh, she was pleasantly surprised when mid-afternoon on Tuesday a text arrived.

Hiya hope you're not getting a better tan than me!!! Not hard!!☺

It was only a few words, just enough to show that he was thinking of her - and that's what counted.

I've been glued to the computer all day!!☺ Hope you're having a better week!!☺

Thinking that would be it for a few days she was even more surprised to get another text late into the evening. The fun followed and she felt their closeness and hoped it sparked something in him too.

Now you've got me at it... Watching these chaps called footballers kicking a ball around!!! So how much do we have to win by then???? Doing my emails in the middle as I'm not that good at sitting still for 90 mins!!☺

This made her smile. The fact that he was showing that he was making an effort to share her world felt wonderful. She had only mentioned that she had watched the football once and he had remembered.

Well done!! Rooney is frustrating me and he needs to come off!! If it finishes as is then England will go through top of table. If France win their game then we'll go through 2nd. Does that make sense?? It's getting tense!!☺

Ahh hhhh?????????? Maybe I'll just flick back to BBC 24 news!!! I get that!!☺☺☺

And then when the game finished, she decided to update him on the outcome to see if he had got it or not.

Great result!! England vs Italy on Sunday to look forward to (providing France don't come back from being 2-0 down)!! ☺ Hopefully you'll be able to get the highlights on News 24 as well!!☺☺

Hey you... I got duff info...Some divvy sounding guy on the telly said they're top of their group and ahead of France...What do they know ehh!!!☺☺

Was he really struggling to understand it that much!! Demi would have to sort this out if they were to have a future.

They are top of their group and ahead of France!! France has now finished their game as they were later finishing then England and the final result wasn't known when I sent my text!! Keep up!!☺

Think I'm going to switch my England support to the woman's volleyball team!!! None of my mates seem to care what the score is!!!☺

Ha ha!! Boys will be boys!!☺

Then suddenly it was Friday again. Getting ready to sit at home and watch the football seemed like the perfect time to text Josh to catch up on his week and his plans for the weekend. She wondered if he was out or not. Well she would know soon enough if he replied to her text.

Hi. Just providing Mum's taxi service then its back home for Spain vs France whilst ironing!! A cracking Friday night!!☺ Hope your week finished well & your weekend has got off to a good start!! Have fun.☺

Later, just as she decided he must be out and she wouldn't hear from him that evening, she received a text.

Hey u I can beat that!!! You're not even trying!!☺ I'm doing my clan's washing whilst watching 'a knight's tale'... 2001!!! Had a nightmare the last 3 days with the banks deciding to threaten the building society sector by stopping all money in and out... Kinda what we do for a living!! Anyway going out looking at houses for most of the day tomorrow. Fingers crossed that the survey on my old house on Monday goes ok – criteria for a new one I think is going to end up being as run down as they come for the money I've got!!☺☺☺

She had heard the news about the banking problems and hadn't thought Josh's line of financial services would be affected by it. She was obviously wrong and Demi would need to develop her financial knowledge if the relationship was going to evolve the way she had planned.

Knowing he was at home she wondered if they could chat for a bit so she set about sending a reply.

Sorry! The competition is too great!!☺ So you win again!! Hadn't realised you'd be so affected by the bank debacle!! Money, Money, Money!! House hunting is great fun! I love looking around other people's houses!☺ Sounds like you could be heading for a bit of a challenging project!!☺ The football has got boring so think I'll channel hop for a bit!! Enjoy the film!!☺

Hey channel hopping ehh... I didn't realise you were such a good swimmer!!!☺

After the mighty Zambezi channel hopping is a doddle!!☺

Texting this brought back memories of Demi's holiday in South Africa. She and Jenny had such a great time and she wished Jenny was here with her now. The accident had happened only a couple of weeks after Demi had returned from South Africa. How awful and very different things would have been if the accident had happened when Demi was on holiday in South Africa. Demi's holiday had come at a good time as without it she may not have coped and survived as well as she had over the last, very challenging, few months.

CHAPTER THIRTY FIVE
Home Coming

A T THE HOSPITAL on Saturday Jaini was told that all was well and the home coming could happen on Wednesday. Everyone was very excited. The boys had completed all the adjustments and the decorating was done.

There were just a few final medical checks to do, physio and a care plan to be put into place. The hard work, worry and courage by everyone had paid off and life could begin to take on a normal rhythm again.

Demi was keen to get to Wednesday, to start the next chapter of life and to help her family move forward with less worry and in the hope that they would experience nothing quite like this again.

Jaini was excited about Wednesday. Yes, she wanted everyone to settle into a new, worry free routine only she was concerned about how Demi would take the news she had to tell her. Jaini had pinned so many hopes and dreams on it; sure that Demi would share these. As it got closer to revealing the 'secret' Jaini got more anxious. Every time she thought about it she could feel something niggling in the pit of her stomach.

Meanwhile Josh, who was oblivious to all of these dilemmas in Demi's life, was keeping spirits up with another text. It was Sunday afternoon and being desperate for some distraction from her thoughts she couldn't help smile at his reference to football.

Hi u what did you do to England last night ehh??☺

She enjoyed the fact that he was keeping an interest in the football and she couldn't help wondering if he felt the same as she did about their relationship or what, if anything, he did feel about it. If he noticed how she did her best to offer some interest or encouragement. Boy, she really was in a philosophical mood! She replied, keeping it short to mirror his, and because of her mood.

Hi. They played well they just couldn't quite finish it off!! What does the week ahead offer for you?☺

She really wanted to tell him about the homing coming on Wednesday and dreamt about how fantastic it would be to invite him to join them. He felt like family to her and it would feel right having him there.

His reply was fun although the information about him going away for a week was a bit of a shock.

I'm away on holiday from Wednesday for a week... Have to get away from all the traumas of house moving. I just need the world to slow down for a bit!!☺

Although shocked, she was pleased he was taking some time out and she genuinely wanted him to have a good time. Her angst came from knowing that this week, with him being away, would give her the opportunity to do what she needed to do. However, for now she focused on her reply and enjoyed their small line by line chatting.

Thank you! I hope you're off to somewhere nice & warm!! Have a lovely time and don't do anything I wouldn't do - therefore the world is your oyster for a week!!☺☺

Hey Skegness apparently can be nice this time of year!!!☺☺ Have to keep off the oysters after I had my fish reaction!!! Apparently they are an aphrodisiac but I think one has to be having sex for it to work!!!☺☺

Wow, that was a brave reference for Josh. Was it his attempt at flirting? She smiled as she imagined the shy grin on his face as he had typed his text.

I think you may be better off packing your wellies rather than your sun cream if Skeggie is your destination!!☺ As for the oysters & sex I'm keeping quiet - for a change!!☺☺

And there was I thinking I could rely on you for words of wisdom!!☺

She decided to leave it there and wait until Wednesday to use her reply to wish him a happy holiday. Would that be her last text to him she wondered?

Wednesday! What a day. What a turning point. Josh off on a week's holiday and her sister coming home from hospital. All this and a 'secret' to be revealed. It was all beginning to feel like all the elements of the universe were aligning themselves for some big explosion.

Everyone was anxious about the hospital home coming and worried about how they would all cope. On top of that Jaini was anxious about her 'secret'. How was she going to break the news?

At least Josh was out of the way for a while and for once she hoped he wouldn't text, at least for a few days. As she thought this she remembered to text him to wish him a happy holiday. She needed to do it quickly as if she had spent time thinking she would have got herself into a spin and she really didn't have time for that today.

Hey, wishing you a fab holiday, safe journey & lots of fun (without the oysters)!!☺☺

The flat was ready for the home coming. Family were in place and a small party was laid out to receive its very special guest.

Demi was sat in the hospital with Jaini waiting for the discharge papers. As soon as the documents arrived they said their final 'goodbyes' to the Doctors and Nursing staff and made their way to the car for the short journey home.

Jaini was amazed at how calmly Demi dealt with everything, taking it all in her stride. Jaini hoped Demi would stay as calm when she told her. She had decided it would have to wait until tomorrow as today was all about getting home. Also they would probably not get any time alone today and tomorrow would probably be their first chance.

CHAPTER THIRTY SIX
Jaini's Story – 'That Day'

THAT DAY, when her world changed. That day, when nothing would be the same again. That day, the day of the accident.

The not knowing whether she would survive or not. The waiting, the pain and the anguish. They had all suffered on that day, not just Jaini and least of all, Demi.

The only thing to survive intact from the accident was her mobile phone. The police had given it to Jaini at the hospital. It had been her only comfort during those long dark hours, scrolling through the contacts. It had helped her feel close to the ones she loved.

She had wondered, at times, whether she should contact the listed names in the phone to tell them about the accident. Then she would remember that they probably all knew by now. Although she couldn't help thinking, what if someone didn't know and really they should know. What if it were the other way around, would Demi know who to contact if she were in this situation?

One late and particularly dark night Jaini had found herself going through the text messages. She needed to feel close to people, people who Demi knew.

She was in a serious condition and the outlook at that point was bleak. This was Jaini's darkest hour. The family were gathered and everyone was pacing up and down, back and forth to the coffee machine and regaling fond stories. Occasionally there were bursts of laughter as funny memories emerged. And then there were the tears that followed as the seriousness of the situation was remembered.

Jaini had remained quiet; the phone had not left her side since the police had given it to her. It was her one and only comfort. The one and only connection she had with her sister. It was during that long dark night that she discovered one particular line of text messages that sparked her interest.

Of course Jaini knew about Josh, Demi had talked of nothing else for months. What Jaini didn't know was that Demi had ended the relationship and was horrified by the final text that she found and what she read into it about Demi's emotional state at that time. Jaini was relieved to read that Demi had seen sense and had attempted to rekindle the romantic friendship, albeit that it was still at an early, tentative stage.

After being rocked and heartened by what she had read Jaini started to wonder what she should tell Josh about the accident or indeed whether she should tell him at all. She was unsure what Demi would want and after agonising for a few hours Jaini decided to wait and see. To wait until they had more information about Demi's injuries and recovery prospects. In the meantime there was a lot more to worry about and agonise over.

The next 48 hours were the longest in Jaini's life. The longest in all their lives: Demi's boys; Jaini's girls; Mum, Dad and the rest of the family. Friends and work colleagues had all been getting in touch and for once Jaini saw a real positive in social media and realised how helpful it was in being able to easily communicate and update people and thank them for being there.

This also niggled at Jaini as she knew Josh wouldn't be included in these communications because he was not connected with anyone in their 'circle' of connections. Not only that, Jaini could recall Demi telling her that Josh didn't use social media at all.

Now that they knew Demi was out of the woods concentration had moved to her recovery, which they had been told could be long term. How she had managed to survive at all was indeed a miracle, for which they could not thank the medical staff enough.

The Doctors were clear that the next few weeks would be difficult and everyone would need to be prepared for the worst. They had not known then whether Demi would be able to walk unaided again or quite how much movement she would regain. The whole family were devastated by the news, yet determined that they would not give in, no matter how difficult it got. They would all be there for Demi to encourage her every step of the way, literally.

Still nagging away in Jaini's thoughts was what should Josh be told, if anything. Surely it wouldn't be long before he would text Demi and what would he think if there was no reply. Demi was not well enough for Jaini to talk to about this so Jaini decided to sit it out for a couple more days and to wait and see what happened.

And then, there it was. One week after the accident, with Demi only just regaining consciousness, a text arrived from Josh. A long chatty one, tinged with its own challenges and sadness, sending Jaini into a real dilemma.

Would it be fair to tell him, as he may feel a sense of responsibility and not know how he should deal with it? This could add to his already challenging life and cause him more difficulties in dealing with his emotions and recovery from his divorce.

If she didn't tell him and ignored his texts it would be weeks or months before Demi would be well enough to respond. By then Jaini was sure Josh would have given up hope on their relationship. Even the thickest skinned person would take a hint like that.

Equally, if Demi's phone had been lost or damaged in the accident then Josh's text, all of Josh's texts, would have been lost to the universe. No-one would have known that he had sent a text and therefore no-one would have responded and Josh would have disappeared from Demi's life, all their lives.

Therefore, was this a sign? Had the phone survived, beyond all comprehension, and come into Jaini's possession for a reason? Jaini firmly convinced herself that this was the case. This gave Jaini a sense of responsibility for taking ownership of Josh's text and Josh and Demi's 'friendship'.

Jaini decided, there and then, before she changed her mind, that she would reply to Josh's text as if she were Demi. She would not tell Josh about the accident as she did not want to add to his anxiety. In time she would tell him. Anyway, it wouldn't be too long before Demi could pick up where she left off and Josh need be none the wiser. That would surely be the best solution that would help them all during that traumatic time.

Convinced that she had made the right decision Jaini embarked on her reply. She and Demi had similar personalities and styles so hopefully Josh wouldn't notice a difference. Jaini was careful to ensure that she put herself as much as she could in Demi's 'shoes' when replying to him.

It didn't take long before Jaini realised that the situation might be getting out of hand. With Demi making such a strong recovery, she could have dealt with having her phone returned and could have picked up on texting Josh if that had been what she wanted.

Jaini realised that as Demi had not asked about her phone that she must have assumed it had been lost in the accident. The thing was, Jaini had not put her right on this. Jaini had not given Demi her phone back nor had she told her about Josh. How could she find a way to do that now?

The longer it went on the more difficult it became. Jaini kept telling herself that she was doing Demi a favour as Demi hadn't been well enough to cope with it. Demi needed to concentrate on her recovery and not get side tracked by a figment relationship.

Jaini knew that the day would come when she would have to tell Demi what she had done. She convinced herself that Demi would be pleased and would thank Jaini for doing this, for caring and understanding. After all, Jaini had done it because she cared and because she knew what Josh meant to Demi and she didn't want Demi to lose that. She had been through too much recently and deserved some happiness to look forward too.

As time went on Jaini decided that she would wait until Demi was out of hospital and back home before she told her what she had done. And the closer it got to that day the more anxious Jaini became. She wasn't as convinced as she had been that Demi would be pleased with what she had been doing behind her back.

Also, would Josh notice the change in style and context of the texts when Demi took them back over? Would Demi continue with the texts? This made Jaini scared as, would Demi continue? Or would Demi stop and then everything Jaini had done would have been wasted? If Demi didn't continue, what would this do to Josh? How would he cope if the texts just stopped? Jaini felt that she had gained his trust and had really developed their relationship to a point where they were almost ready to meet.

The more Jaini began to think about it, now in the cold light of day, she became worried about how first Demi and then Josh, would react. She began to realise that what had started out as something innocent and with all good intentions, could now be interpreted as stupid and damaging.

She began to realise that Demi may well feel betrayed, let down and sad that she had lost out on a relationship that Jaini was hiding from her. And then, there was Josh, he too could feel betrayed, robbed of reality and a friendship he thought he had.

At best Jaini could hope that they may at first react badly, and she would understand and accept that, and then gradually they may begin to understand that Jaini had acted out of love, worry and hope. Maybe she shouldn't have gone on with it for so long and maybe she should have told Demi about it before now, especially as Demi emotionally had been well and coping for a few weeks now. However, Jaini hadn't wanted anything to upset, hold back or hinder Demi's recovery. Jaini wanted the best for Demi, that's all she had ever wanted and she hoped beyond hope that they would know that and understand.

Jaini had thought long and hard about when and how she would tell Demi what she had done, for her. She had finally decided that she would sit down with Demi when she returned home, having been discharged from hospital. Jaini was very excited about this day as well as having a feeling of anxiety about how Demi would react.

As the home coming day approached Jaini's emotions were stretched to the max. Excited about Demi's home coming she was busy making sure that the flat was decorated and ready for Demi. She had organising the 'home coming' party and had made sure the family were prepared and in place ready to welcome Demi back into their world. Jaini was anxious about when the right moment would present itself and how she would start the conversation. And now that she had over thought it, Jaini was worried about how Demi would react and what that may do to her.

It was the day after the 'home coming', after all the friends and family had gone and the tidying up was done, Jaini and Demi found themselves alone together with time to sit with a coffee and contemplate the next few days. Jaini was updating Demi on the list of friends who she knew were planning to drop in. Jaini had been in touch with them all to arrange a bit of a plan so that Demi didn't get too overwhelmed too soon. Demi needed a little time to adapt to her new surroundings and limitations, although these limitations would only be short term, she still needed time to adjust.

It was during this discussion that the situation presented itself. Jaini sensed the opportunity and decided if she didn't take it then she may not have the courage or opportunity again. She needed to do it and do it sooner rather than later.

As Jaini began to tell Demi, she could see the emotion develop in her eyes. Jaini had not anticipated this reaction. The emotion was intense and far outside anything Jaini had dared to believe or think.

CHAPTER THIRTY SEVEN
Demi's Story – 'Loss and Hope'

IT WAS A FEW days after coming out of her coma before Demi was able to start piecing her life back together. Recalling much of the details about life before the accident took time. She had no recollection of the accident itself; what had happened immediately before it or anything about afterwards.

The police had been in and spoken to her a couple of times. They had told her that the accident was not her fault and that no-one else had been injured. They said that the lorry had skidded on some oil on the road and had gone out of control. The lorry driver was fine, apart from being badly shaken and very concerned about Demi. All in all it was a miracle that she had survived and that no-one else had been hurt and for that she was truly grateful.

The police had returned her personal items that they had found after the accident and Demi had been slightly disappointed, although not surprised, that her mobile phone was not among the returned items. She didn't bother to question it and accepted it for what it was.

Demi's family had kept her up to date with all the lovely messages that had been sent and kept on coming in from friends, colleagues, acquaintances and other family. These were great to receive and really helped Demi to keep positive and focused on her recovery. However, for Demi there was something missing, someone missing and she was at a loss without her phone to do anything about it.

Demi had some very long, lonely times where she reflected on things. When she could go back over her life and appreciate it for what it had been. Remember people who had come in and out of it and the influence that they'd had on her. Josh had been one of those people. He had entered her life, not just once; their paths had crossed three times now, at very different intervals. Thinking back to the first time, which was difficult to pin point the exact moment as it was during the time when they had worked for the same company, Insurance 4 U. Demi had joined Insurance 4 U fourteen years ago and had worked there for three years in total. During that time she and Josh had worked together a few times, although she would not have described them as close colleagues. He was the senior manager of a department that Demi supported with people and staffing issues.

The second time their paths had crossed was some six years later and completely out of the blue. Demi hadn't even noticed him sitting a few tables apart in that small, out of the way coffee bar. He had clearly noticed her though! And he had taken the initiative to do something about it, when he could have just left without saying anything. How little did either of them know how important the impact of that meeting was to have on their lives? It had only lasted about thirty seconds. Enough time for Josh to say hello, take Demi by surprise, and hand her his business card.

The third time their paths had crossed, how bazaar had that been? How bazaar had been the events that had followed? That balmy September evening with hundreds of other fun seekers enjoying the late summer warmth. It was incredible how he again had spotted her. And, how disappointing it was that he had disappeared without speaking to her. How brave had she been to follow this up with her phone calls to him. Clearly there was some bond between them for these brief encounters to have happened and for them to have maintained such a friendship over text messaging.

Although Demi would have loved their relationship to have been closer and more personal she had understood Josh's position and anxiety and felt that they had a mutual understanding and respect. Demi had accepted this while living in hope that one day their relationship may move to a different level.

What Demi had not anticipated was the bombshell that had been dropped when she had returned from her holiday in South Africa. Demi loved her job and was pleased with the way that she had structured her career and the path that she had mapped out for the future. Her world had been completely shattered at that fateful meeting on her return to work. She had no idea how she was going to recover from it and believed that life, as she had known it, had ended and anything that was left would soon be destroyed when word got out about it. Rather than have Josh find out and put an end to their relationship, Demi had preferred to take matters into her own hands and finish it herself before having it done to her. It was that line of thought that had led her to send Josh that text to end their friendship and any chance of a real relationship.

Demi was at her lowest point ever then and having never experienced anything like it before she had no idea whether she had the strength or energy to pull herself through. The things she did have though were her family and two very special friends, Jenny in South Africa and Dyna, her colleague. And between them all they gave Demi the hope and positivity to keep going. That is what had encouraged her to re-text Josh a couple of weeks later and gave her the strength to carry on, to rebuild and believe in herself.

Demi couldn't remember the exact point when she fell in love with Josh. It was early on in their texting relationship during one of Josh's dark and difficult times when she realised that she wanted to be with him, to hold his hand and to show him how much she cared. Demi knew that this love was only first stage love as without actually being with Josh she knew that what she was in love with was at a superficial level. She knew that there were more stages of love to come as and when their relationship progressed and became personal. She loved what she had already and was in love with the prospect of what was to come. Demi had hoped and wanted Josh to feel the same way.

That was before her life had fallen apart. While her love for Josh had not altered she knew that he would never be able to fall in love with her after that. How could he? He needed someone strong, credible and professional. Demi had lost all that then. She had believed at that time that ending their relationship was the kindest thing that she could do for him.

It was only with the support from her friends and family and their encouragement to get Demi rebuilding and believing that enabled Demi to realise that she had maybe been a bit hasty in ending their relationship. Maybe she should have trusted in him, as he had no idea what had been going on in Demi's life, yet she had chosen to punish him for it.

Demi wouldn't blame him if he didn't respond to her 'revival' text. Would she respond if she were him? He made her wait a bit before he did and she was so excited, more than she had ever admitted to herself. Although, it was hard going and she wasn't sure that they would be able to get back to where they had been before. And that was when the accident happened and Demi's live changed dramatically, again.

When Demi had come out of her coma and spoken to the police, there was no mention of her mobile phone. Demi had accepted that it had been lost, having no reason not to. Demi realised straight away that her phone was the only way she had of contacting Josh or him being able to contact her. Without it they had no other method of contact. She had no way of letting him know what had happened. He would be waiting for a text from her and would be wondering what he had done or what had happened to give reason for her not to reply. This filled her with huge sorrow and sadness. However there wasn't anything that she could do about it so she would have to let it go. Her broken heart was just another thing to mend along with all the other broken parts of her body. She knew that it would be her heart that would take the longest time to recover. It was also all out of her hands, there really wasn't anything that she could do. In any event the last thing Josh needed was her to worry about and feel a responsibility for. It really was better to just leave it.

She missed him. She knew she missed him as she thought about him every day. There hadn't been a day since she had regained consciousness from the accident that she hadn't thought about him. Wondering what he was doing; who he was doing it with. Tormenting herself with imagining him with another woman, that woman, who had no sense of fun or adventure.

She had worried about him, wondering how she had hurt him and how long he had waited for her to reply to his texts. How long had it taken him to move on or how badly had she added to his scars.

However with Jaini's revelation this was at least something Josh had been saved from, for now!

Demi wasn't sure how she felt when Jaini began to reveal her story. She wasn't angry. In a lot of ways she was pleased, particularly that Josh had been spared all the hurt and emotion that Demi had been visualising and agonising over.

Demi knew Jaini and knew that Jaini would have acted in what she had thought at the time was the best thing to do.

Knowing Jaini, she knew that once it had started to snowball she wouldn't have known how to change things. Jaini would have been worrying about it for a while and would have been panicking over doing the right thing and deliberating what the right thing to do was.

Demi had no idea how to deal with this. She remembered Jaini saying something about Josh being away for a few days. This would at least give them space to think.

Demi was curious, what did Josh think? What was Josh expecting to happen next? How had their 'fictitious' relationship developed over the last few months? What dramas, emotions, stories had been going on in Josh's live that Demi was supposed to know about? How had Demi responded to these? Had she been appropriately supportive, sympathetic and sensitive? Had Josh noticed any change in her approach to him? What had Jaini said and committed Demi to honouring?

Demi realised that she needed to see and read all of the texts that Jaini had sent. She needed to know what Josh had been doing, to understand how he had coped and what he had been going through. She needed to know how Jaini had dealt with this. To see how Jaini had balanced humour with sensitivity. This wasn't something Jaini was always so good at.

Despite all of her anxieties about what Josh had been going through and how Jaini had dealt with it, Demi realised that her relationship with Josh was at least still alive. That was something Demi could cling on to, that would give her hope. Demi knew she wasn't angry with Jaini. How could she be, after all Jaini had done and had been through these last few months? In fact, when Demi reflected calmly on the situation, she was thankful that Jaini had taken the trouble to do what she had. Without it Demi and Josh's relationship would have been over, just as Demi had thought it was.

Now there was hope, reality, and Demi knew, deep down, was something that could only bring happiness. There was only one thing in the way and that was Josh, and how he would react when she told him what had happened. She owed him that much, didn't she?

Demi began to smile and then to laugh. The laughter turned to excitement as she started dancing around, albeit limited in her condition. Demi reached out and hugged Jaini, thanking her for what she had done. Jaini was completely taken aback and it took her a few seconds to realise that Demi was genuinely happy. Together they laughed and cried with joy and excitement. Then they settled down to talk about what their next move should be. How and what they were going to tell Josh. Whether they were going to tell Josh?

CHAPTER THIRTY EIGHT
Josh's Story – 'Passion and Pain'

AS SOON AS Josh returned from his three week, 'fix your life' holiday he knew what he was going to do. First on his list was to get his phone and second, to text Demi. He needed to know how she was and what had prompted her to end their relationship in the way she had. He needed to know for sure if she really was no longer interested. If so, he would deal with it. If not, then he did not want to give up without trying. He needed to be sure.

As soon as he was able to he grabbed his phone. Quickly scanning through the many missed calls and messages he spotted Demi's name. Puzzled he opened the text.

PLEASE READ.....On my return from holiday I was presented with a serious work situation that I found difficult to deal with initially. My reaction to this prompted my last text to you. The situation, whilst serious also provides a number of opportunities that I am keeping optimistic & positive about – nothing much keeps me down for long and there is always something good that comes from everything if you look for it – This was just a tough one for me to get my head around for a few days. I am sorry that I did not tell you this before and for making the assumption that I should end our friendship as a result. I have really missed your texts and I would really like them to continue. I will understand though if you decide not to reply. I hope that you will at least accept my apology for the abruptness of my last text and that you might understand a little about what was behind it. Thank you for reading. Take care and best wishes. D

He wanted to cry, laugh, jump up and down, reach out and hold her, all in one go. He was ecstatically happy to hear from Demi yet desperately sad at what she had told him. All he wanted to do was to be with her. Then he noticed the date she had sent the text and was horrified that it was almost two weeks ago. She must have been thinking that he wasn't bothered and he wouldn't blame her for that. Why had he let them talk him in to leaving his phone behind? He knew he should have taken it with him.

His well-conceived plan was now out of the window. He needed a new strategy and he needed to respond to Demi, pronto. He decided to rewind his thoughts and play it slow, to ease them back together gently. He needed to test how she was coping and how vulnerable or how strong she really was, as clearly she had been through a tough time, and had dealt with some tough issues.

It hadn't taken them long, as within a couple of weeks they seemed to have picked up where they had left off and Josh was enjoying their contact. He sensed that Demi was struggling at times and was amazed with her ability to keep going and to keep offering help, hope and good spirits towards others, putting them first. He was worried about who Demi was getting support from and yet didn't feel she was ready for that to come from him. He wasn't sure she was strong enough to have a real relationship in her life at that time.

And he wasn't fully convinced if that was because of his own vulnerabilities or because of Demi's. He knew he had a complicated life and he didn't think it was fair to bring Demi into that just now.

Instead he had decided to go back to enjoying their friendship by text, developing their own 'text affair'. He hadn't wanted that to end, he knew that much. He also knew he wanted more, yet felt prepared to wait a bit longer for it, to make sure that they were both in the right place. He knew it wouldn't be long before they were ready and he knew that when the time was right it would have been worth the wait.

Josh was very busy at work over the next couple of months or so. He was out travelling to London and around the country regularly each week. In any of his spare time he was house hunting to find the perfect place for him and his girls, where they could settle and call their own. His divorce was all sorted and the matrimonial home about to be sold. He was able to move on with the rest of his life and support his daughters in getting their lives and futures back on track. They were good girls, having been through a lot and had managed to get through it fairly unscathed. They had their own career plans and josh was excited about what the future held for them and being there, watching and supporting them with it. If he could have Demi by his side at the same time then that would make his life complete.

Despite his busy schedule, Josh had managed to keep in close contact with Demi and felt that they had become more spontaneous, with their texts being sent at all sorts of times and days, with some serious, some flirty, some fun, with a good balance, just like a real personal relationship. Well almost!

It wasn't long, having been so busy, before Josh needed another break away from it all. He had managed to schedule in a well earnt week off. He wasn't going far, just up to a north England seaside town for a bit of light rest and relaxation. He planned to do some walking, sightseeing and mingling with the locals. He had an old school friend he had kept in touch with who he was going to meet and share some 'old boy' laughs and jokes. In many ways he wished he could have invited Demi to go with him as he would have been far more excited about a week in a north England resort if he was spending it with her. If he had his way that would be the last time that he took time off on his own as he was intent on building a future with Demi and spending the whole of the rest of his life with her, not just a short week.

Josh had told Demi that he was going away. There were no guarantees what sort of phone signal he would have so he had wanted her to know that he wasn't avoiding her or being rude. He couldn't risk any wrong assumptions being made and he definitely did not want Demi upset or worried.

He wasn't surprised to receive Demi's text early in the morning on the first day of his holiday. He was warmed and chuffed. She was always so thoughtful and caring. Having that thought started Josh reminiscing about the times they had spent together at Insurance 4 U. The times he looked forward to their meetings, enjoyed the playful banter they always had. He would watch out for her as she walked through the office to the canteen each morning to get her caffeine fix. She was so elegant, smartly dressed, calm and confident without any inkling of the emotions she stirred up in him and probably more than half of the other hot blooded males in the building.

He hadn't believed his eyes the day she had walked into that back street coffee shop some years later. He had spotted her straight away; it was as if the whole world had frozen except for Demi walking through the door. He was completely thrown in the conversation that he had been having and had needed to be jolted back to reality. She hadn't noticed him as she ordered drinks and spoke to her colleague. Not wanting to miss the opportunity he had summoned the courage to speak to her and give her his business card. He felt like a bumbling fool and she was as polite, friendly and lovely as he had remembered. She had accepted his card and smiled at him gratefully for taking the time to say "hello". He had then immediately wondered in hope whether she would contact him and cursed himself for not finding out more about her, in case she didn't.

After a couple of weeks of not hearing anything from her he had gone back to the coffee shop in the hope of bumping into her again. In fact he had gone back to that same coffee shop regularly for weeks in the vain hope that she might appear before his very eyes, again, and that it would not be the same recurring dream that he had been having most nights.

He knew that when they had worked together at Insurance 4 U that she was married, as he was. When they met at the coffee shop he could not tell, and had no idea, if she was still married. He knew that he was and he knew that his marriage was going through difficulties and he wasn't sure how much longer it would survive.

Over the next couple of years after giving up all hope of ever seeing Demi again he had done his best to keep his marriage going. However, the cracks had gotten deeper and the sticking plasters were no longer strong enough to hold them together.

Bringing himself back to Demi, Josh recalled that the most bazaar time that his and Demi's paths had crossed had been on that wonderful Friday night in September. He had been completely mesmerised when he saw her walk into that bar. So mesmerised he couldn't take his eyes off of her for one second. His mates had teased him and he had tried to ignore them. Demi's friend had spotted him staring at her and had told Demi, who had looked straight across at him. Their eyes had locked and he knew at that moment that their lives would intertwine, he just hadn't known quite how.

With the deep cracks that had appeared his marriage, it had become unrepairable and it had ended with things being incredibly acrimonious, with his daughters being caught up in the middle of it all. Josh had always been known for never doing anything by half and his split with his wife had definitely fallen into that category. Josh knew that his mates would not be impressed if he told them about Demi. They were still in protective mode and had dragged him out for a drink to cheer him up a bit and give him some company outside of the four walls he had been staring at for the past few weeks.

Seeing Demi had definitely cheered him up. Having to not say anything to his mates and walk out without speaking to her though had left an empty void.

Suddenly bringing himself back to reality and realising the time, Josh bundled himself into the car and set off on his long trip North. It wasn't until later when he had finally arrived and settled into his accommodation that he remembered that he hadn't replied to Demi's text wishing him a happy holiday. That didn't mean that he wasn't thinking of her, as she was constantly in his thoughts.

It was the weekend, Josh had only been away for three days and he felt torn, torn away from Demi, which felt strange, as they weren't together anyway. Yet he felt miles away from her when all he wanted was to be with her. He knew that the only thing between them was a text from him inviting her out. He would have to do this. He needed to know how she felt and he needed more from their friendship. He needed to know if they had a real future, together.

Josh decided there and then that he would text Demi. He would be back home on Wednesday and back to work Thursday and Friday. He had no plans for that weekend so that would provide an ideal opportunity.

Before he could deliberate any further or change his mind he wrote the text that would define the rest of his life, their lives, and he pressed send.